PENGUIN M...

THIS LOVE THAT FEELS RIGHT...

Ravinder Singh is the bestselling author of *I Too Had a Love Story*, *Can Love Happen Twice?*, *Like It Happened Yesterday* and *Your Dreams Are Mine Now*. After having spent most of his life in Burla, a very small town in western Odisha, Ravinder is currently based in New Delhi. He has an MBA from the renowned Indian School of Business. His eight-year-long IT career started with Infosys and came to a happy ending at Microsoft where he worked as a senior programme manager. One fine day he had an epiphany that writing books is more interesting than writing project plans. He called it a day at work and took to full-time writing. He has also started a publishing venture called Black Ink (www.BlackInkBooks.in), to publish debut authors. Ravinder loves playing snooker in his free time. He is also crazy about Punjabi music and loves dancing to its beats.

The best way to contact Ravinder is through his official fan page on Facebook, at https://www.facebook.com/RavinderSingh.official. fanpage. He is more frequent in his response to readers on his Twitter handle @_RavinderSingh_.

C000202894

This
Love
that feels
Right...

RAVINDER SINGH

Penguin
metro reads

PENGUIN METRO READS

USA | Canada | UK | Ireland | Australia
New Zealand | India | South Africa | China

Penguin Metro Reads is part of the Penguin Random House group of companies
whose addresses can be found at global.penguinrandomhouse.com

Penguin Random House India Pvt. Ltd
7th Floor, Infinity Tower C, DLF Cyber City,
Gurgaon 122 002, Haryana, India

First published in Penguin Metro Reads by Penguin Random House India 2016

ISBN 9780143423027

Typeset in Bembo by Manipal Digital Systems, Manipal
Printed at Replika Press Pvt. Ltd, India

www.penguinbooksindia.com

To Ankur Sharma, my first personal trainer in the gym. A jovial and good human being, I learned a lot from him. This one's for you, Ankur. My guru dakshina!

My name is Naina Singhania.
I am twenty-five and I am married.
In my life, marriage happened first and I fell in love later.
The only problem was—I fell in love with a man who's not
my husband.

This is my story . . .

~

One

On that afternoon, driving up the spiralling ramp connecting the basement car park to the exit, I lost my newfound confidence as a driver. It was my first time driving up a steep incline. The problem was not so much with driving up. It was that I was stuck behind a car which had abruptly stopped. Damn! I cursed, as I applied the brakes.

The car in front of me had just begun to move when it halted again a few feet ahead. I tried to do the same. But I failed miserably. You see, the second I released the brake to press the accelerator, my car began rolling backwards. Reflexively, I hit my right foot back on to the brake paddle. The vehicle immediately came to rest. Phew!

I realized this was going to be tricky. You need to be quick with this whole shifting from the brake to the accelerator thing—I told myself.

I took a deep breath and went for it again.

The second attempt was unlike the first. The first had been better.

I shifted from brake to accelerator effortlessly, but I fumbled while releasing the clutch at the same time. This juggling was challenging enough for me on level ground, this time the race was also against gravity! It was quite a circus!

It required understanding, experience and a cool head—none of which I possessed at that moment. My car continued to roll back. I panicked and slammed hard on the accelerator. The engine roared. Time for me to release the clutch gradually, I reasoned. But I couldn't control the action and ended up releasing it in one go. The vehicle jerked forward and came to a dead halt. The ignition went off. I was back to square one. No, actually, I had rolled back and was further down from square one.

The next second I looked into the rear view mirror and my fears came true. Another car had just arrived, right behind mine.

Shit!

I hated being in that situation.

All this while, the car in front didn't move an inch. It must have been waiting for other vehicles to move. Stuck at a turn in the ramp, I could not see beyond the car ahead of me. But I could hear the sound of the engines and their accelerations.

At that moment, how I wished that one of the cars would break down to buy me more time. But they only broke my heart. They moved!

When the car in front moved the world behind me expected me to do exactly the same. But I was on a slope! On a spiral slope! On a spiral slope with a car standing inches behind mine!

Plus, my previous two failed attempts were still fresh in my memory.

Mother Earth, swallow me!

All this while, I had been pressing hard on the brake. I reignited the engine. I was quick with this part—twisting the key and infusing life into my car—having mastered it through numerous repetitions during my driving lessons.

Suddenly, the car behind me honked. And then, there were a few more honks, one after the other. In the rear view mirror, I could now see a trail of cars. *Shit!*

It was time.

Just do it, Naina!

I looked at my moist fingers trembling on the steering wheel. Sweat beads appeared and rolled down behind my right ear. I swallowed the lump that had formed at the back of my throat. I felt sick. I wanted this to be over as soon as possible.

'I have to do it. I HAVE TO DO IT!' I psyched myself.

And then to my car, 'Okay clutch done. Now, first gear . . . okay . . . now . . .'

'Maataa raani bachaa lena!' It is now all up to you, Goddess!

And then I let go . . .

Two seconds later, I felt the thud. The front of the car behind me was dented, its number plate bent. And guess what? It had a temporary number on it and its white, pearl-finished body was glowing under the ramp lights.

Even the Goddess had not saved me.

~

'W-H-A-T? You rolled back into a brand new car?' Manvika appeared to be shocked before she burst into laughter. She was thoroughly amused listening to my ordeal from the day before. I wasn't sure if she was laughing at the situation or at me. I had become quiet and when she saw my sad face, she stopped.

'Oh sweetheart, I was just imagining the whole scene!' she said, still grinning and trying to control her laughter as she adjusted the edge of the towel she was wrapped in.

The two of us were in the steam room.

I noticed how comfortably she had called me sweetheart, given that we had only got introduced to each other an hour back, in the basement of the mall. I hadn't found a place to park my car in that jam-packed parking lot. I was in an argument with the parking lot attendant, who was trying to get me to park my car in the open parking beside the mall, when Manvika stepped out from her car. She had arrived just ahead of me and taken the last available slot, I suppose.

'Hi,' she said from a distance and walked towards us. The guard made a face when he spotted her. Perhaps, she was a regular in this mall.

I instantly recognized her even though it was the first time I was seeing her in sportswear. Her stylishly permed hair, which was thick, black and short, accentuated her oval face. It helped me recall who she was. She didn't look as tall as she appeared on the TV screen. I guess her sports shoes made the difference; she would be in stilettos in her show. Yet, if not 5 feet 10 inches she must have been around 5 feet 6 inches, at least an inch taller than me. But she possessed a fit body with just the right bust, something her business formals enveloped nicely.

'Either you free up those reserved slots . . .' she said pointing her finger at the space right next to the elevators, demarked by temporary barriers, denoting they were reserved for some exclusive guests in the mall, '. . . or let me speak to your boss so that I can complain to him about how the parking for differently abled people is being misused by some of the regular visitors with your help.' She now pointed at the space beside the elevators where there would be a wheelchair sign, which was no longer visible.

I watched how in a matter of seconds the attendant's face had turned pale. For a moment he was at a loss for words. His tone changed to worry and he immediately offered to help me find a slot. Manvika had nailed it. She smiled at me. I wanted to tell her that I knew her, but right then my first priority was to park my car. 'Thank you so much!' I said and followed the guard.

Moments later, as I was waiting at a gym's reception area for a sales person to attend to me, I bumped into her again. Earlier, her attire had already made me guess that she might be heading for this gym.

'Hey, you found a spot?'

I happily nodded and asked, 'You are Manvika Thakral, right?'

I had watched several of her 8.30 p.m. debates on Newsline, a popular news channel on TV.

'Oh, so you know me!' She smiled.

I introduced myself and we spoke briefly, as she was about to start her workout. But then she suggested that perhaps we should catch up after our workout. Even though she had said it casually, I felt obliged to meet her for what she had done for me back in the parking lot. And as it happened we landed up together in the steam room and started talking.

She was in no hurry and I had a lot of time. And with no one around us in that steam room during that time of the day, we eventually ended up having a long conversation.

Since she'd helped me in my moment of crisis, I ended up telling her about my previous day's experience, which coincidentally took place in the very parking lot.

'I feel sorry that it was a brand new car. I only realized when I stepped out of my car to see what I had done. He was already out of his by then,' I said shamefacedly.

'He?' Manvika asked with a twinkle in her eye.

I blushed. 'The guy in the car behind me,' I clarified. 'Forget what you are thinking. I was petrified and I had to keep apologizing even before he could say anything.'

'Okay, then did he abuse you?' she asked concerned.

'Nope! Surprisingly he didn't. He was very calm.'

'Really? That's odd . . .' Manvika said, with disbelief in her voice.

'Yes. In fact, not only did he not shout at me, but when he found out my problem, he offered to drive my car up the ramp from where I took over.'

'W–H–A–T?'

By now I could barely see Manvika because of the thick steam between us.

'You lucky, beautiful girl!' she teased.

I blushed again. I knew the point she was trying to make. On the one hand she made me feel good about myself, but on the other hand, I didn't agree with the logic with which she was trying to connect the dots. At first, I thought I would let it pass because we didn't know each other very well. But then I thought otherwise.

'He didn't have a choice!' I blurted out.

'What was he like?'

'Hmm . . . tall, about 6 feet. Well built. He wore a cap matching his red slim-fit T-shirt along with a pair of straight fit denims and sneakers . . . I guess . . . yeah! He was dressed casually . . . but smartly . . . it's just that . . . I found his wearing the cap a bit strange. Not sure if the trend of wearing caps is still in.' I told her what I could recall of the stranger.

'I wouldn't find that strange as long as it goes with the attire. In fact my trainer wears a cap too. But tell me this—he wasn't upset at all? I mean this was his brand new car, right?' Clearly, she couldn't rationalize his reaction.

'Oh, he was. I could see disappointment on his face. But then he didn't lose his cool. That was quite amazing of him. At the spot where he left my car and handed over the keys to me, I even offered to get his car fixed,' I replied.

Manvika quickly asked, 'And what did he say then?'

'He said he would claim the insurance.'

My answer made her think.

'Such a gentleman you drove your car into!' She chuckled and clapped stirring the steam between the two of us.

'I felt guilty. I am, even now! I wish I could have done something for the damage I did to his car and the hassle he must've gone through because of me.'

'Come on, Naina! It's okay. You apologized and you offered to get the car fixed. What more could you have done?'

'Hmm . . .' I sighed. But he did not take the help I had offered, so I still felt guilty.

Neither of us said anything for a while. The vent made an abrupt noise and began flushing gallons of steam again. The temperature that had fallen a bit by then began to rise. I pushed my head back and relaxed waiting for the steam vent to turn silent again.

'Do you think he didn't get mad at you but helped you because you are beautiful?' Manvika asked as if she was interrogating me.

I realized she had an inquisitive nature. I guessed a lot of it had to do with the profession she was in.

'Beautiful? C'mon! You're being nice to me. I'm plump. Besides, you are undermining his intentions.'

'Well, you have a beautiful face with sharp features and gorgeous skin. Your long dark hair complements your fairness.

I am not being unreasonably nice to you. As far as weight is concerned, you have joined this gym to lose it. It will happen. Eventually!' she said.

'Thank you for saying that but I wish, I could be bold and fit—the way you are.'

'Ha ha! Well, I shamelessly accept that praise. Thank you! But I want to know why you said . . . I am bold?' she asked.

'Mmm . . . not just bold, but the entire attitude with which you carry yourself . . . I really admire it.' I didn't know what it was about her that was making me very straightforward with her. The way she had been protective about me, paid attention to what I'd gone through, made me want to tell her everything even though this was our first long conversation.

'Attitude? Well, what exactly in it?' she asked. She wanted a more objective answer.

'Hmm . . . like the way you carry your news debates. You are precise. You articulate your point so well, in fewer words. And you are brutally honest.' I paused for a second. She was quiet so I spoke, 'I never found you hesitate in calling a spade a spade, no matter who is on your show. You are direct. And this no-nonsense stance of yours is what I admire the most. It is commendable. Not sure how you do it, but all this makes me, and I am sure a lot many of your viewers, like you.'

I didn't hear her react. I couldn't see her reaction. I could just feel her strong silent presence. I'd thought she would be very happy to know my opinion of her. But nothing of that sort happened.

When she finally spoke she said, 'Anything that you don't like or hate in me?'

That was not what I'd expected, but I answered anyway, 'Can't think of any.'

She whistled. 'Awesome!'

'Ha ha, now you say that!' I laughed. 'I'm not lying, you know.'

'I know. Thank you very much for your compliment,' she said in a reassuring tone. She meant it.

And then the ten-minute timer we had set for our steam session went off. It was time to go out. As I stepped into the cold shower I thought about the stranger on the ramp. I remembered his smile.

I smiled too.

Two

The next morning was beautiful! At least to me it was. Sunlight streamed through the sheer curtains of our apartment and I could hear birds chirping in the distance. As I lay in bed next to Siddharth, I reminisced about the happenings of the day before. I turned to look at Siddharth and put my hand on his chest. I realized it had been long since we'd been close, really close. I had to wake up Sid for his golf. He would be gone all morning. But I didn't feel sad. I was happy. After all, I had something exciting to look forward to in the day. The idea of going to the gym promised to fill the void in my days.

Siddharth yawned and turned his head towards me, adjusting the pillow with one hand. He placed his other hand on mine and looked at me.

'Not getting late for golf, Husband?' I asked.

He picked up his mobile phone from the side table. It was six.

'Yeah! I'd better get going. My friends would be waiting,' he said in his husky morning voice.

He was about to get up from the bed when I locked my hand in his hand and pulled at him. He looked back at me.

'*Arey!* What happened?' he asked surprised.

I looked at his face for a brief while and then smiled and said, 'Nothing!'

I released his hand. And he walked straight into the attached bathroom.

As he got busy getting ready for his golf, I wondered if he would enjoy a morning workout in the gym with me. Husband and wife running on the treadmill next to each other sounded like a fun proposition in my mind. I thought I would talk about this idea with Sid. But before that, I would have to check what time the gym opened in the morning.

~

My session at the gym had been the same as the previous day. I stretched and warmed up after which I did about forty-five minutes of cardio. And then, just like the day before, I ended up finding Manvika in the steam room.

The steam vault had just gone on snooze mode. In the silence that occupied the next couple of minutes, Manvika found the opportunity to go back on the subject we had just digressed from previously.

Clearly, the guy's reaction to my blunder had tickled Manvika's thought buds. She was not through with that conversation yet. The steam had begun to settle down. In the yellow light of a bulb the visibility in the room was partial.

'So what do you think about that guy? Why did he react in the way he did—could it be because you are beautiful?' Manvika asked wiping the water off her arms and adjusting her posture.

I don't know why she was still stuck on that subject. I could not help giggling. Honestly, it was a bit strange for me to talk about him with Manvika.

'You must be thinking *haath dho ke peechey pad gai main!* That I am just not letting the topic rest,' she admitted.

And I decided to respond to her with the same straightforwardness, 'The beauty of the person at fault won't compensate for the losses of the one who has incurred them. So the way I look is not going to make up for the damage I did to his car.'

'Interesting argument!' Manvika said.

'Argument?'

'I am a news anchor you see! This vocabulary is an occupational hazard,' Manvika clarified. Then she added, 'But good looks do raise expectations . . .'

'Expectations, what expectations, Manvika? You know that I am married.' I smiled.

'Does it matter?' Manvika responded while unwrapping her towel that had come loose across her body and draping it back. She didn't mind baring her body to me, even though it was for a second or two. Perhaps she was comfortable doing so in the mild fogginess that pervaded the room due to the steam. I noticed a tattoo on the left side of her waist. It appeared to be a scorpion crawling down.

'Shouldn't it?' I asked, trying to focus on our discussion.

For some reason Manvika didn't answer that. Instead she asked, 'But how would he know that you are married?'

I looked at my finger and recalled that I had placed my ring in the locker during the workout. I had feared that the pulley pushdown cable would rub the shine off my ring during the exercise.

'I was wearing my ring,' I said.

'Hmm!' Then she affectionately said, 'Ironically, the ring won't make you look less beautiful.'

'It certainly makes me appear forbidden, I guess,' I was quick to respond.

'And the forbidden fruit is so sweet, my dear,' she said, grinning naughtily.

I laughed.

'What about you, Manvika? Are you married?'

'Yes, I am,' she replied.

We had been debating for a while now. But I felt alive. *That's the beauty of holding a discussion with an intellectual like Manvika,* I thought. She could quickly present a completely opposite point of view and make it sound logical. I had just begun to enjoy our discussion when someone opened the door. I suddenly became conscious of my surroundings. The outside air rushed in and the clouds of steam dispersed. The temperature dropped again.

Two ladies wrapped in towels stepped inside. Amidst the fog they took a few seconds to adjust their eyes and notice the two of us, after which they found places to sit. I wish they had not entered the room at that moment. Manvika continued with the conversation, completely ignoring the presence of the two other ladies.

'So wouldn't you agree with what I said?' she asked.

There was no way I was going to continue though.

'I don't know what you intend to prove, but it will be interesting to carry on this discussion tomorrow. I have to leave now. Else, I'll be late.'

She clearly sensed my discomfort. 'Makes sense! But I am not here to prove anything. I am a seeker, rather. A curious person who is often looking for answers.'

'Sure!' I got up to redrape my towel, as I prepared to step out for a shower.

As we got out of the steam room, Manvika reminded me of the personal trainer programme in the gym. About half an hour previously, in the changing bay of the ladies' room, she had told me that she had opted for a personal trainer programme. As per the programme, she had a dedicated instructor to train her. 'It's a more professional and goal-oriented programme,' she had told me back then.

I recalled that the day I had visited the gym for the first time the sales person had spoken to me about it. But I had not shown any interest—as long as there were enough floor trainers to help me I didn't need any fancy trainer watching my every move!

But Manvika was all praises for the personal trainer programme.

'It's really good. It keeps you focused. I achieved my goals faster than I would have otherwise. Check with the front desk. Aarav, my trainer, is quite good,' she said.

'I will,' I promised before leaving.

Outside the ladies' room, I bumped into a familiar face. The recall wasn't instantaneous. I had just deposited my used towel and turned back when this happened. We sort of blocked each other's way. I immediately moved right. So did he. Then he moved back left. And so did I.

I got nervous. I looked at him.

Underneath a sporty navy blue sleeveless jacket, he wore a collared white T-shirt. Navy blue trackpants and sports shoes completed his look. Over his jacket, closer to his left chest, was his name on a label. In that split second rush to give way to each other, I failed to read the name on it.

He looked at my face trying to figure out something and then immediately said, 'I am sorry,' after which he stopped moving and made way for me. I nodded and smiled as I walked away.

I guess he smiled when we passed each other. I imagined it was a mysterious one. One that I had experienced earlier. One that had made me nervous before.

I kept my eyes glued to the ground and yet there was not a moment that I wasn't aware of him. I knew I had seen him before! At the glass doors near the reception, I turned back, now almost sure of where I had seen him before.

He too turned around. We were now looking directly at each other. He was still smiling. My heartbeat grew faster. My eyes must have told him that I had recognized him. *Yes! It was him!*

It suddenly struck me that I should reach out to him and ask if he had got his car fixed. But before I could do so, he waved his hand at me, turned around and left for the men's room. The back of his navy blue sleeveless jacket read— Personal Trainer.

Three

'Today was my second day at the gym.'

It was a little before midnight. My husband and I were sitting around the dining table. I had eaten already. He had just begun his dinner.

It had become a routine by now, one that included his returning late from work. His evenings were either consumed by office work or by cocktail meetings in hotels, where he networked with fellow builders, high-profile agents and his investors who fell in the abbreviated leagues of NRIs, HNIs and CXOs. On some occasions he would also have the company of bureaucrats and politicians. I could divide his networks into two kinds, one who had money and the other who held power. These connections were of prime importance to my husband. After all, he had to take his real estate business to heights that, according to him, I could never even imagine.

'. . . the one that's in the mall . . . on the opposite side of the road!' I said, still trying to grab his attention.

He was busy reading something on his phone. Must have been a work-related email.

'Hmm . . .' was all he said. He didn't look up.

Siddharth, my husband, is a good human being, as well as an intelligent businessman. I know that. He inherited the values of a traditional Indian family from his parents—a trait my parents had liked a lot in him. No wonder, when the proposals for my marriage had started coming our way three years back, my father had preferred him over others. I got married quite early in comparison to the rest of my batch-mates. I had always trusted my father and my family to make the right choice for me on my behalf.

Our fathers were business friends. And as they wisely matched us, Siddharth and I transformed their business friendship into a relationship.

My husband has always been a soft-spoken individual. In the two years of our marriage, we have hardly ever fought and I can't recall him ever being loud. But then when one person has learned to compromise with the other, where's the need to fight?

While I grew up as my daddy's girl, Siddharth is a mama's boy. He would never talk back to his mother and had immense gratitude for her, so much so, he came home early from work if she merely made a call. If I made that call, I was refused with valid reasons.

Siddharth accepted that he counted himself blessed to have an understanding wife like me. He often said that to me as well. While my father-in-law had passed on his business responsibilities to his son, the home front was still ruled by Siddharth's mother. She had the willingness, time and energy to retain the essence of their family lifestyle, something Siddharth admired about his mother. And because Siddharth is my husband, I ended up liking all that he admired. Sometimes, I tried to recall what I used to really like before my marriage.

'Siddharth!' I said a bit impatiently.

He raised his finger, indicating that I should wait a bit.

I sighed grumpily. I wanted him to pay attention to me, to ask me how the gym experience had been and whether I had faced any problems. But that was something I could not expect from Sid. *Was it because we'd not fallen in love before marriage? Did people who were in love with each other behave like this?*

Ever since my college days, I knew that I was fated for an arranged marriage. There was to be no love in my life. To fall in love one needs to be in a place where love can blossom. When did I have that opportunity? I wasn't even like my friend Deepika who insisted she would have a love marriage and announced it to her family as well. We used to laugh at her. Who could decide when to fall in love? How could she be sure she would?

Where I came from, the chances of love happening were close to zero. I didn't live in a hostel. I wouldn't travel in the metro to college either! Neither was I on the back of bikes, holding on tightly to guys and talking as if the world didn't exist. In my life was a driver and a luxury car that would drive me to my college and back home. I wished my dad and mom would have been less protective. I hardly went out with friends and fellow students. My weekends were spent with family, watching a film on our home theatre system or having dinner with family friends.

I would hear about affairs and attractions when my friends talked about the films they'd seen together or the mall they had hung out in. Their weekends were fun. My Sunday mornings would start with a puja at our ancestral temple. On certain weekends, when we didn't want to come back home, we would either go to our Chattarpur farmhouse or go on a weekend getaway to any nearby resort. I was away from all that my friends called a 'fun weekend'.

I was different from the rest of the girls in my class. They could wear anything they wanted. In our house Daadi, my fiery grandmother, had reduced my choices to salwar suits. Only when I got my father to intervene, did she half-heartedly allowed me to wear jeans and other Western clothes. Although even then she was clear that I could wear my sleeveless tops, skirts and shorts only in the house and that too in the absence of male visitors.

Yet, I loved Daadi and my entire family. Because everyone cared for me, even my little brother who is seven years younger to me. Had my Chachu, my father's younger brother, not moved to settle in the US, I would have had his daughter, who is about my age, to share things with. So I didn't have any friends at home either. I certainly had been the apple of my dad's eye, but then, in the traditional air of our home, he wasn't supposed to become my best friend. I looked at Siddharth. He could have been my friend.

'Siddharth! I want to talk to you. Please listen *na*,' I shrieked.

'Just gimme a minute, Naina,' he said and I made a face.

It had always been like that. I had to wait. Sid has always been an ambitious man. He is the third generation in this family business in the Delhi–NCR's real estate sector. While my father-in-law had inherited the business from Siddharth's grandfather and expanded it greatly, Siddharth's dreams were much more ambitious. He wanted a faster and a much bigger growth, that too in record time. He had often told me about the way his father and grandfather used to run the business and how he intended to run it differently. Even I could see the difference in Siddharth's way of management from that of his father's.

Armed with an MBA from a prestigious B-School, my husband understood the importance of being a branded real estate builder very well, especially the importance of investing in publicity. In contrast, the only focus his father and grandfather had was how to keep the spending low and maintain the standard profit.

'Why incur expenses in doing so many things? Just invest in land,' his father would say. He feared needless spending in publicity and advertising could lead to losses. It made him restless when Sid didn't listen to him. And sure enough, over a period of a few years, Siddharth was able to ultimately show profit in the balance sheet. His father showed his happiness and pride by handing over nearly the whole of his business to his son.

That's when the Hindi-speaking, old-style office made way for English-speaking smart executives. With that began a new era for Singhania Constructions Pvt. Ltd. The number of employees of the company also grew from forty-five to close to two hundred people.

I got the flavour of Sid's passion for business immediately after our marriage, when at the very last minute he postponed our honeymoon by fifteen days. A few of his NRI investors were visiting India during that time. How could he miss this opportunity!

Postponing his honeymoon to make way for business, in my mind, only verified what my father had to say about him— he has the talent to become a well-known business tycoon! My father was right.

Only, I wished he had not been this right.

I didn't regret the delay in our honeymoon. I only wished Siddharth had asked me for my opinion and involved me in the decision-making process as well. I would have felt valued.

In hindsight, it turned out that the postponement was worth it. The NRI investors did invest in Singhania Constructions and this fact added to much happiness in our postponed honeymoon. But then, all this was two years back.

'Sid . . .'

'Yes *baba* . . . I am listening now. Tell me . . .' he said, his eyes still glued to the mobile screen.

'No, you are not,' I said pouting.

He didn't react. I stood up and walked up to him. I stood behind him and put my elbows on his shoulders.

'Why did you marry me when you were already married to your business?'

This was not the first time he had heard this from me. This was not the first time he had so conveniently ignored it either.

He turned to look at me after which he locked his phone and kept it over the table.

'This was important,' he said smiling softly. 'Tell me now, what were you saying?'

I looked at him and into his eyes, trying to see myself, trying to measure my share of place in his life. *Was I even there? Why did it feel like a mistake asking for his time?*

'Naina! Speak now,' he said and folding his sleeves pulled the dinner plate towards himself.

I closed my eyes for a second to let go of my thoughts that had become a routine these days.

'Remember, I told you in the morning that I will be visiting this gym in the mall in front of our society?'

'Hmm . . .' He nodded as he ate.

'I quite liked it. I am going to work out there . . .'

'Good! Go ahead then.'

That was not what I was expecting. I wish he would have asked more about it. I wish he'd taken some interest in talking about it.

'Actually, I was thinking if you too could join along with me. Right now I go during the day. But if you come along we can work out in the morning. At six!' I said, already apprehensive enough of his reaction. 'It's a very nice gym, supposedly the best in Gurgaon.'

But it didn't make any difference.

'Come on, Naina! Where is the time for me to do all this? You know I enjoy my golf.'

Of course! Any other answer would have been a surprise for me. Golf was also a part of his networking. It fitted perfectly with his ambitions.

'Hmm . . . how about alternate days then?' I insisted just for the sake of conversation.

He took a sip of water and swallowed. 'No, baba! I mean look at me. I am fit. My routine works for me. I don't need to go to a gym.'

I wish I could have told Sid that perhaps getting up together in the morning and working out together would bring a new joy to our lives that had otherwise become so monotonous. We could be together for a while, away from this home and work, and get some time that we could truly call our own. But he had already finished his side of the argument.

Then I reasoned with myself, why should I worry about getting up early in the morning? It made sense for me to join the day slot which included a couple of other homemakers. I could make new friends in that circle. I already had a great start by meeting Manvika. At least I would be able to spend a few hours of my day doing what I enjoyed.

Four

The ceiling of the gym was carved in a zig zag shape with bright lights installed in the protrusions. It offered quite a view when one was lying on one's back on the yoga mats and looking up. Speakers at various corners of the walls were installed close to the ceiling.

It was quite a high-tech gym. Most of the machines had display panels that gave a hell of a lot of information, which I didn't even know how to comprehend. My membership card looked just like an ATM card. It had a chip in it to mark my attendance and to open my locker in the ladies' room. There were iPads installed in the aisle next to the juice counter. If you looked at one you would find a YouTube workout video or a leftover Google search on healthy diet. The entire length of the wall in front of the treadmills had a series of LCDs installed on it. The screens were not simply wall mounted but kind of embedded into the wall with a big glass screen over them.

People could change the channels from the panel on their treadmill. On the rest of the cardio machines the display panel itself had an inbuilt TV screen. No wonder it was called the best gym in entire Gurgaon. Equally high was its membership fee, probably the highest in Gurgaon. But then the amenities offered made it worth it. Everything about it was grand and luxurious.

'Madam, you can scroll through and let me know who you would want to choose,' said the sales person helpfully.

I stood in front of a touchscreen LCD, mounted on the wall next to the cycling bay. The blasting music added life to the gym. It was my third day at the gym and I was looking for a personal trainer as suggested by Manvika.

I had just arrived at the reception and told them that I wanted to know more about personal training sessions. And in no time, I had become a lead for one of the sales guys, who had been called to the reception desk. A tall, thin guy presented himself for the sales talk. He walked me to the nearest screen on the wall. All this, in less than one minute and thirty seconds of my arrival in the gym! I was quite surprised and impressed at their speed.

So there I was. Viewing the thumbnail display pictures of over a dozen personal trainers who trained in the gym. It all appeared much like an overhead display of the menu in a pizza shop. All the faces looked the same.

'Who would you like to go with?' asked the sales person.

'Wh . . . what?' *Am I supposed to pick a trainer myself. Well, how do I zero in on one?* I thought.

For me, the even bigger problem was to take the call amidst so many people working out around me. The idea of scanning pictures of well-built men in public made me uncomfortable. It was awkward. *What if right now these trainers are secretly watching me from a distance and wondering who I'll choose? Shit!*

'Is this how people choose personal trainers here? By looking at their photographs?' I asked the sales person unable to hide my shock.

'No, madam! You can look at their profiles by clicking on their pictures. It's a hyperlink. I will show you,' he said and tapped a random picture on the touchscreen.

I was embarrassed enough having to scan the muscular men on the screen, now I had to tap my fingers on their pictures in order to read their profiles!

The profile talked about the area and level of expertise, achievements (if any), years of experience, weekly schedule and available time slots along with lesser relevant details of each and every trainer.

I was certainly not willing to go through all the profiles one by one. And if I had to pick a few, I wondered if it was all going to boil down to their looks. Weird thoughts came to my mind. I missed Manvika at that moment. I looked here and there, wishing I would spot her so that she could rescue me from this strange situation.

'I mean I . . . I don't know . . . any of them? How can I judge, merely by seeing their pictures and profiles on this LCD?' I asked. I'm sure I was looking even sillier than I thought I was.

However, the sales person was smart enough to understand my inhibitions. He had probably read from my body language that I wasn't one of those very confident girls who knew exactly what she wanted. He therefore offered to help me further.

'Okay, let's apply some filters and reduce our options here,' he suggested as he tapped with his fingers on the screen.

'Most of our women clients prefer to go for functional training. I hope you too would be interested in it?' he asked.

'What's that?' I asked since I didn't know what it was.

'Hmm . . . one of the forms of exercise to get in or retain being in shape. It's not the regular weightlifting that mostly men go for—the bodybuilding, the dumb-bells and the bars . . . you know,' he explained.

Even though I couldn't clearly picture it in my mind, I became relaxed at the thought that it didn't involve bodybuilding and lifting heavy weights. And the point that most women go for it to be in shape was a relief.

'Okay,' I answered.

'Perfect! And should I look for morning slots for you?' he enquired.

I nodded and said, 'Yes, during this time of the day.'

He applied the filters. A list of six trainers appeared on the page. And then it happened. I found a familiar face. I had bumped into him. Twice! The circumstances notwithstanding. And given the self-conscious state I was presently in, it was a relief to see him again.

I wondered how I'd missed his face in the previous displays.

One familiar face among the unknown crowd brings a lot of comfort, even if it is of a person you barely know. That day, this fact made the difficult task of choosing one from among the many trainers marginally easier for me.

Aarav—it read underneath his picture. *Nice name! Whose name did Manvika take when she talked of the personal trainer . . .?*

The sales guy kept talking about the trainers, but I guess I had made up my mind for two reasons. I realized that even though there was enough written about every trainer, practically I knew nothing about them. In such a scenario, at least I knew that this Aarav guy was a nice human being. The perception was based on a real-life event, which again had been very recent. Besides, by availing of his training services, I could genuinely do some good to him in return for his helping hand the other day. And if by any chance he wasn't good, I would opt for a different trainer in the subsequent month, I thought.

As I zeroed in on my choice of personal trainer in my mind, the sales guy spoke again, 'Madam, should you be interested, I can arrange a trial session for you to see how it goes with your trainer. You need not pay for it.'

Trial session! Wow! With that, the sales guy had put all my concerns to rest.

'That would be great!' I said as I pointed out the trainer I had opted for.

He then asked me if I would like to go and change for the trial session. Meanwhile, he would get Aarav for me. I readily agreed.

About ten minutes later, I sat beside the juice counter, inside the gym, waiting for my would-be personal coach to arrive. The juice bay was strategically located towards the centre of the gym. It had a few round tables along with a few chairs around them to sit on with health magazines and newspaper dailies kept on them. A coffee vending machine sat right next to the counter. I saw a few folks taking black coffee out of it. I guessed it was for free as no one paid.

The place offered a great view of a major part of the gym. Even though I had been there a couple of times, I was not familiar with the whole area. Till then my awareness was limited to the largest section of the gym, the cardio zone with its long array of treadmills and cross-trainers. This was where I burnt my calories the day before. Awaiting my trainer, I took a closer look at the rest of the area. There was a weightlifting zone with all sorts of dumb-bells in the rack and bench presses. Next to it was a soundproof group classroom with a maximum of the wall facing inside made up of glass, thereby offering an exciting view of the people training. There was no one in there now. But on my first day at the gym, I had happened to see and admire the high-energy group workout in there. I realized there were defined time slots for the same.

'He has just finished his workout and has gone to take a shower,' the sales person updated me from a distance. In the meantime he offered to buy me a smoothie from the juice counter, which I gracefully declined. 'I'm okay, I'll wait here,' I told him and he left. I picked up a health magazine from the stack that lay on the table in front of me. I flipped its pages and stopped on the ones that I found interesting.

'So we meet again!' A voice broke into my reading. I looked up. It was him.

'I am Aarav,' he said.

'Oh, hi! I am Naina,' I said standing up from my chair.

'No! No! Please keep sitting,' he said and grabbed the chair next to mine. He was wearing his personal trainer jersey, the one he wore the day before, along with his cap. Only now, in our first comfortable meeting and proximity, I observed how his veins, originating somewhere above the half sleeves of his T-shirt, ran under the skin on his big forearms. 'That's the result of his workouts,' I told myself.

'Listen . . . listen I . . . I am very sorry for what I did the other day . . .' I had only begun to apologize one more time, when Aarav cut me and said, 'It's okay, madam! It's been taken care of. My car's all fixed now.'

I felt relieved that we had it out of the way before our first formal discussion.

'So tell me how can I help you? I have been told you want to go for personal training?'

'Ah, yes! Manvika, my new friend in this gym, told me about the concept of personal training and . . .'

'Oh, she did?' Aarav again cut me mid-sentence.

'You know her?' I asked

'I train her,' he said smiling. His eyes narrowed in an attractive way when he said that.

'Oh!' So this is *him*! In that moment I wondered how she would react when she got to know that the brand new car I backed my car into belonged to her trainer. I felt amused at the thought. Manvika would definitely laugh too, given that she had deep interest in why the guy didn't react the way she thought he should have.

'Great! I don't see her around today?'

'She didn't come in today. It's her rest day. I generally, take Sundays off. I try to. But it depends from week to week. Otherwise, I train Manvika on alternate days from 10 to 11 a.m.'

I recalled that Manvika had told me that her trainer was quite good. I realized that accidentally, I was on the right track.

'That means you won't be able to train me in this slot of 10 to 11?' I confirmed.

'Well, yes! I can either train you on the days when I don't train Manvika or I am available for the 11.30 to 12.30 slot,' he offered.

I got busy wondering which slot I should opt for. But Aarav broke my thought process and said, 'You can decide it later as well—after you have taken the trial session. But we can only do the trial session tomorrow, as I have only twenty minutes left with me, before I begin my next session. I had already committed to that one,' he said looking at his wristwatch.

'Oh, that will be great,' I said.

'Meanwhile, let's get to know where you stand as on date and what you expect out of this training.'

'Ah! One question!' I interrupted.

'Sure!' he acknowledged.

'What comprises functional training?' I asked out of curiosity.

'Hmm . . . how about I show you the functional training zone right now but explain it on the day we start it?' he offered.

I thoughtfully nodded my head.

'Come!' he said getting up from the chair.

I followed him to the extreme left end of the gym on the other side of the reception desk.

Predominantly, it was an open area with various pulley machines installed in the corners. A lot of hand-held equipment and gym mats were stacked beside a big wall, the placard on which read: Functional Training Area. *So this is what the sales person was referring to!* I thought.

'All that you see in here—the bosu, the kettle-bells, the plyometric, the resistance tubes . . . all these comprise functional training.'

It all sounded Greek to me. But at least I got familiar with the equipment I was going to lift . . . or pull . . . or whatever.

'Have you recently checked your BMI?' Aarav asked.

'What . . . I?' I asked, failing to understand what he'd said.

'B-M-I,' Aarav repeated.

I looked at him blankly.

He smiled. His eyes became smaller. My heart started beating faster.

What was happening to me?

'Body Mass Index,' he said looking at me.

'Oh! Okay!' I nodded my head still not comprehending what it meant. I assumed Aarav wanted to know my weight and was throwing a technical term to impress me. I had already subtracted my actual weight by 2-point-something kg. On second thoughts, I took the liberty to round off the 2-point-something to a whole number of −3. Ah! That would sound okay if he asked.

But Aarav busted me. He moved a little closer to me, looked straight into my eyes and said, 'You didn't get it, did you? It's a part of your body composition report.'

And all I heard was the loud thudding of my heart in my chest.

Five

I managed to catch my breath and apologize. 'I . . . I . . . I am sorry, I don't know what that is. Is it some kind of test?' I was scared that it had something to do with needles.

'We do a body composition test to find out things such as muscle mass, fat mass, percentage of body water and waste to hip ratio in one's body,' Aarav answered.

'And you don't need . . . a . . . my . . . I mean . . . my . . . my blood sample for it. Right?' I stammered.

'What?' Aarav looked at my frightened face. 'No!' he chuckled.

I sighed with relief.

He laughed. 'No blood, no urine, no clinical stuff. Relax! It just involves taking physical measurements. In a way, the process is similar to when you measure weight,' he clarified.

'Oh, I see! No, I've never taken this test.'

'Let's take it then and get you started? We can utilize the brief time I have with me before my next session,' Aarav said and waited for my response.

'Sure.' I smiled. I still wasn't comfortable but I guessed there was no way out of it.

He began to walk. I had to follow him.

On our way we passed the men's and ladies' rooms on my left, separated by a space with a giant window from where the members collected fresh towels and deposited them back after use. Crossing the reception desk we arrived at the cycling bay. And right next to it was a tiny secluded room, which appeared more like an office space. I figured we were heading towards it.

'Er . . . you're following me, right?' asked Aarav, breaking my chain of thoughts.

'Yes,' I nodded smiling sheepishly and continued following him like a kid.

On the way to god knows where, he asked me when I had had my last meal and if I was yet to do my warm-up.

'I ate breakfast about an hour and a half back. I am yet to do my warm-up.'

'Great!' Aarav said pushing the wooden door of a tiny room on his left.

'But why would you ask?'

'An already warmed-up body or a meal taken too recently will lead to incorrect results,' he explained, opening the door and holding it for me, without looking at me. I was impressed.

As soon as I stepped inside the room, the door shut behind me.

And suddenly, I felt disconnected from the rest of the gym, the crowd outside. To be in that little closed room along with Aarav had instantly made me conscious. I was in close proximity of a man I barely knew.

'Okay,' I said. I must have surely sounded nervous but he didn't bring it up. I was grateful for that.

'That's the body composition machine, madam,' Aarav said, pointing to a technical-looking machine. There was a panel and platform over which I was expected to stand. It had the left and right footmarks labelled over it. As I approached it I noticed that the panel had a small display. Two metallic arms emerged from underneath this panel.

I looked around. There was a table to my left—two chairs placed on either side of it. Some papers and files were lying on it. Aarav went and sat on one of the chairs. Then he got busy looking for something. My eyes fell on what he had pulled out from a drawer attached to the table. It was a measuring tape. *Shit! He did talk about measurements! And the waist to hip ratio stuff! Oh god!*

Did he also mention bust? Shit . . . shit! He is going to measure my body! In this small room with no one else present!

'Excuse me! Isn't there a female instructor in this gym?' I blurted. I was too nervous.

Aarav gave me a puzzled look.

'Aaa . . . Yes! There are two,' he said after taking a moment.

'Okay,' I said, but I was unable to convey my thoughts clearly. I hoped I had dropped a hint at least.

'You want to meet them for anything specific?' Aarav asked.

'Ah . . . perhaps, I . . . think . . . I . . . can . . . take . . . their . . . help . . . you . . . know . . . for . . . the . . . measurements,' I hesitantly said looking at the measurement tape on the table.

Aarav shifted his eyes from my face to the tape that he had just pulled out of the drawer and placed on the table.

'You want measurements?' he asked looking back at me.

I could not make out what he meant when he asked that.

'You pulled out the tape,' I pointed out.

'Ah!' He laughed and said, 'I was pulling out things from the drawer in order to find a pen.'

I laughed nervously. This was embarrassing.

Naina, run out of this room! Right away!

'Right! Right! Right!' I repeated and tried to nod convincingly and at the same time maintain a poker face to hide my embarrassment at my stupidity. 'But outside you did mention measurements, didn't you?' I tried to sound intelligent.

'Yes, your height and weight,' he answered. Then he felt something was amiss. 'Are you all right, madam?'

'Yes! Yes! Yes!' Again I repeated. Quite consistent with my stupidity!

Aarav asked me to take off my shoes and socks. I did. Soon I was stuck with my back to the wall, when Aarav adjusted the bottom of the wall-mounted scale over my head.

'And your height is . . . let me see . . .' he said and added, 'five foot . . . . and . . . mmm . . . six . . . no . . . five . . . inches.'

He then asked, pointing at the body composition machine, 'All right, madam, can you please step up on this machine for me?'

I carefully placed my feet on the designated foot marks on the platform. The display panel immediately revealed my weight. I did not get the option to subtract it by 2-point-something kg (or round it off to 3). Aarav punched in my recently measured height when the cursor on the display blinked. And as if the entire body composition exercise had to become a series of embarrassing moments for me, the cursor now blinked at the age field.

'Your age, madam?' Aarav bluntly asked without any sense of hesitation in his voice.

For some awkward reason, I don't know why, I chose to punch the numbers myself on the panel this time. My body language demonstrated the oh-allow-me-to-take-the-pain-

and-finish-these-little-tasks gesture, perfectly. Not only that, I further tried to hide what I was punching in as if it was my ATM PIN. And yet at the same time I pretended as if I didn't intend to hide it at all! I tried to act smart by focusing on the keyboard. In that moment of slight panic what I forgot to keep in mind was that the display screen revealed all that I had punched in!

Naina, this has been a terrible day for you!

One more thing got added to my list of stupid things done that day. Aarav had witnessed it, and yet again like a gentleman, he didn't react and saved me the embarrassment. He allowed me to be in my stupid space. Or at least, I chose to think so.

Was there a possibility of the trainer declining to train his client because she was too dumb? Did this ever happen in here?

Later, I stood holding the two arms of the body composition machine. It took about ten seconds to analyse and process the inputs. In the end it printed out the result.

'All right, madam, we are done. Let's go out and discuss this report,' Aarav said, his eyes on the sheet.

Finally!

Once out of that tiny room, we took the chairs surrounding the juice bay. Aarav explained to me the minute details from my report.

Some of it made sense to me, while the rest I knew I would understand with time. I was only keen on knowing the percentage of fat in my body and what should be the right amount for me. But that didn't stop Aarav from explaining everything. In the end he said, 'Let's set your goals now. Hmm?'

'Sure,' I replied.

'Well, tell me then?'

I wondered if Aarav was expecting me to say anything other than mentioning my desire to shed some kilos and correct my weight. I looked around at the numerous people slogging in the gym, and wondered about their goals.

'Don't we all have the same goal?' I asked.

Aarav laughed and explained, 'Not really! Someone is here just to get in shape for her upcoming marriage, so that the designer lehanga fits her well. For somebody else, forty minutes of cardio is a part of his lifestyle to keep obesity and related diseases at bay. Not everyone has a weight-loss goal. Guess what! Some people are here to gain weight and compete in bodybuilding competitions. A bunch of people love the Zumba and aerobics classes and see that time as exercise plus fun. Besides, they may not like working out alone. I know of people who want to make their bodies flexible, while others want to increase their strength and endurance. So, you see, there are many goals. Now tell me, what's your goal?'

And in no time, my goal appeared so clichéd in front of the others'. It was going to sound quite ordinary. Hence I chose words that sounded intellectual. It was a sophisticated gym with English-speaking trainers who knew about technicalities like BMI.

'Fitness!' I said. 'Fitness is my goal.' At the back of my mind, I was happy that I had been able to speak in a straightforward way.

'And what's your definition of fitness?'

'Fitness . . . hmm . . . to . . . me . . . is . . . like . . .'

Can we leave now?

'. . . to . . . be . . . fit . . .?' I finished and shrugged. I kind of avoided eye contact with Aarav.

Such a simple word and so difficult to define! I never realized this until I had been asked to explain it.

Somebody please call me on my phone and drag me away from this discussion!

'Wow! That helps!' A smile broke out on Aarav's lips while he nodded his head.

This time, I could not hold myself back at his reaction. And for the first time, I let go of my embarrassment and laughed at myself. And then I laughed at all that I was up to that day.

The best part was Aarav joined me too. I guess it was more to make me comfortable than anything else. And when that happened, I said, 'I can add more to it.'

'Then do it,' Aarav offered.

I felt so relieved. So, I talked more. 'To look fit. To feel fit.' And resumed laughing.

Aarav showed me the thumbs-up! With both hands!

'That's me. What's your definition of fitness, Mr Trainer?'

'Well, it's certainly not as profound as yours, madam. I therefore fear it may not sound as interesting to you, as yours appeared to me.'

When we settled down, I said, 'Yes! My stupidity doesn't have competition.'

We laughed some more at that.

'No, but seriously, please tell me what's your definition of fitness,' I insisted.

Aarav recovered his demeanour and answered my question, 'It's the ability to carry out daily tasks and routine physical activities without undue fatigue.'

I pondered over what he had just said and realized it was an apt definition, which summed up everything very well. My would-be trainer didn't only possess a great body but also had a great mind that synthesized crystal-clear thoughts. *Quite impressive!*

He noticed that he had moved me with his words. But even before I could admire his intellectual quotient, he confessed, 'That's sort of a universal definition of physical fitness. I didn't think it up but inherited when I was reading up on fitness.'

'Which is perfectly fine! We all learn,' I said, appreciating the fact that he was not only well read, but also an honest man.

'Further to this definition, there are five important components to physical fitness,' he said. When I looked curious, he wrote them down one by one on the backside of the report he held in his hands.

'Cardiorespiratory endurance, muscle strength, muscle endurance, flexibility and body composition,' he read out and smiled.

'Great. Thanks,' I said.

'Should I explain them . . .'

'Yes please!' I said eagerly.

'Cardiorespiratory endurance is the measure of our circulatory and respiratory systems' ability to deliver oxygen and nutrients to and eliminate waste products from cells.'

'English please?' I said making a face.

'I was coming to that,' he said smiling.

Such a cute trainer!

'Basically, it means to be fit enough so that you don't get breathless too easily. Let's say if you run for 500 metres at a certain speed and get breathless, your next fitness goal should be to cover 1 km at that very speed before you feel breathless. That's called improving your cardiovascular endurance. Exercises performed over a time with low to moderate intensity such as aerobics, running, etc. strengthen your heart and lungs. They delay the stage of breathlessness.'

'That made sense. Being fit should mean not getting breathless too soon. Yes!' I paraphrased.

I was now keen to understand the other components as well. I liked Aarav's scientific approach to fitness. In my mind, a gym coach's image, till then, had been limited to someone who assists in lifting weights—basically picking and placing the weights and dumb-bells back on the rack. But after my first formal interaction with Aarav and witnessing the atmosphere in this gym, I was looking forward to quite a different personal training experience.

'In plain English, muscle strength is the ability of a muscle, or say a group of muscles, to exert force against resistance . . .' Aarav began to explain the second component.

I listened, but a part of me was also looking at him—the way his eyes crinkled, the way his expressions changed, his body language, soft but firm, and then his voice . . .

Shut up, Naina! Pay attention!

We talked about endurance next and I was happy to note that I had a question, 'But how is endurance different from strength?'

'Well, endurance is about sustenance. It's about how long your muscle, or say a group of muscles, can continue to exert force. You see, strength is about exerting a great amount of force but for a very limited period. Like pushing a sofa in the drawing room or lifting an LPG cylinder in the kitchen. Notice, the duration here is tiny. But take for example, holding a baby in your arms for about fifteen to twenty minutes. The weight isn't heavy this time but the duration is longer. This is endurance. These are examples of day-to-day life where we land up demonstrating fitness.'

'Hmm . . . And what are these?' I asked shifting my finger to the remaining points on the paper.

'Flexibility,' Aarav announced. 'That your body can move through its entire range of motion without pain or stiffness.

For example, can you touch your feet without bending your knees? It has nothing to do with your muscle strength or endurance, or cardiorespiratory endurance for that matter.'

I have already done too many blunders. I would definitely try it at home, I thought. And as we chatted I couldn't help but think about how graceful he had been when I had bumped my car into his. Unknowingly, I had begun to rely on him from that day and I was happy I was going to choose him as my personal trainer.

That afternoon, on the chairs surrounding the juice counter, Aarav and I discussed and set my goals. I explained to him what I was looking for. My wedding anniversary was about eight months away. I wanted to lose weight and look gorgeous by then. I also told him that I was fast heading towards XXL in my clothes and that I hated it. I wanted to reduce and go back to the weight of my college days.

Aarav happily gave a name to my goal. 'Size-M'—he called it. 'In eight months' he wrote underneath it on the back of the BMI report. He then broke this long-term goal into short-term ones. He planned my diet and the related workout routine. I was okay with going to the gym all seven days in the week. But Aarav insisted that I work out five days.

'Your body needs rest. To recover,' he said.

'Roger that, coach!' I acknowledged in a confident and euphoric tone.

'I will see you tomorrow then,' he said and stretched his hand.

I extended mine for a handshake. The next BMI was planned a month from now. *I'm sure I'll be in a better position.*

As I walked out and said bye to Aarav, he looked up from my papers and smiled that smile.

It's my first day of working out with Aarav.

After about seven minutes of brisk walking on the treadmill, my body has warmed up. I am ready to exercise. At the juice counter, Aarav has been reading the newspaper, waiting for me.

I walk up to him. I am excited. I look forward to executing what we had planned a day before.

'Good to go?' Aarav asks me the moment he notices my arrival at his table.

'Yes!' I nod in enthusiasm.

'Great! Let's begin then.' He stands up, folds the newspaper and places it back on the stack from where he had picked it.

'Come with me,' he commands.

I follow him to the other side of the gym, towards the functional area.

We stop by the black–yellow belts that hang from overhead horizontal bars installed connecting opposite walls.

'After the warm-up and before the workout, it's important to stretch,' he says and goes on to explain how it safeguards the body from any muscle injury during the workout.

I listen to him carefully and register stretching as a prerequisite to working out in my mind.

'This is TRX,' Aarav tells me as he holds the belts in his fists and demonstrates what I am supposed to do.

He places his left foot ahead of his body, stretches his arms out, nicely parallel to the floor, and leans in his upper body to the front. His feet are firmly placed on the ground.

The next moment, I follow suit.

I try to stretch my chest muscles. But then my posture isn't exactly what Aarav wants me to hold. He takes the TRX belts from me and shows me how to do it, one more time.

I fail to do it, one more time.

I am not sure what exactly is wrong. It looks fairly simple when he does it.

In order to help me, Aarav places himself behind me.

'Madam, don't drop your elbows,' he says and at the same time places his palms underneath my elbows.

I sense his touch on my skin. A chill runs through my spine, which I try hard to conceal. This is the first time Aarav has touched me. I didn't see it coming. I wasn't prepared for it. I was busy figuring out the right posture.

Aarav's hands on my arms disrupt my focus. I am not used to a man's touch. Not of ones that aren't a part of my family, or even extended family for that matter. This is a strange feeling.

No, it's not a bad touch at all. In fact, in the life situation I am in, it is a much-needed genuine one. It's a touch between a trainer and his client. But then, it's also one between a man and a woman. And I'm aware of it. I can't say the same about him.

Aarav continues to explain something to me. But his voice has become a background sound now. Nothing registers in my mind, except the consciousness that I am being touched by a man I haven't known for long.

Still, it's not an uncomfortable feeling. But then I'm not perfectly comfortable either. What is it then? It's something complicated. Something that's not normal for me. It has left me aware, very aware. It's different. And I am unsure whether it is positively different or negatively so. It's vaguely different. Aarav is not at fault. There is no fault here. He is only doing his job. I am the one who has availed of his services. I am the one who needs to upgrade my mindset. I realize I have to get used to it.

'Do you feel it, madam?'

Aarav's slightly louder voice breaks through my thoughts and I have to pay attention. I guess he has repeated himself this time.

I nod my head in acknowledgement, worried that I might say something irrelevant.

'You should feel the stretch in your upper chest, close to your shoulder,' he tells me.

I focus on the said anatomy part and realize that I am indeed feeling the stretch. 'Yes, I am,' I say this time.

After holding the posture for about ten seconds, Aarav drops his hands. 'Relax,' he says.

My body does. My mind can't.

Six

He rolled over me and woke me up from sleep. His hands caressed my body. I didn't let him know of my disinterest. He went ahead and concealed his face in my neck. His lips were on mine and his arms held me prisoner. Then he began to kiss me all over my face and neck. It was always the same routine. He undressed me. That's how Siddharth was. He didn't need time to get into things, he just did them. I didn't stop him, even though I wasn't in the mood at all. Soon I felt him entering inside me.

That he needs me lessened my discomfort with the whole situation. Probably it was his way of saying that he loved me. Once again, it didn't matter what I wanted. I was happier to be wanted. *How had the desire to be wanted grown to such an extent?*

It must have been in the wee hours of the morning when we made love. No! Not we! When *Siddharth* made love. I simply surrendered, in spite of the fact that what my body desired in that moment was sleep. When he was done, I washed myself in the bathroom and was in bed again—this time with my arm across his body while his back was towards me. I could hear him snoring a bit. *He must be* tired, I thought.

For a while, I could not sleep. My thoughts went to the gym, to Aarav. I recalled the way he had touched me earlier in the day. How that too had come unannounced, just like this one. Yet, unlike the very recent touch of my husband, that one gave me goosebumps. Even though I had felt conscious at that moment, that touch wasn't against my wishes. The intentions behind these two touches of two different men were very different. And they triggered completely opposite responses in the depths of my heart. The non-sensuous one aroused me and the one that was meant to be sensuous was . . . well . . . dead!

Then my thoughts took me in another direction. *Was this the right way to think? Am I turning into a bad woman? The characterless one?* This sudden introspection disturbed me. I pulled my hand from over Siddharth and squeezed it with my other hand in between my thighs. He didn't turn and bother to reclaim it. He was already asleep to notice the change.

I kept comparing the two different touches, while guilt continued to spill on my thoughts and spoil the fun. I don't remember when exactly sleep took over.

The next time I opened my eyes, Sid was almost ready for his game of golf. He took full advantage of staying on Golf Course Road. Even though the golf course was hardly a five-minute walk from home, the driver used to report early in the morning primarily to carry the kit for Sid, as well as drive him from and back home.

The knock on our bedroom door woke me up completely. Sid first looked at the wall clock and then at me. He smiled and mouthed the words, *'Bhaabhiiii, memsaab bula rahi hain . . . (Ma'am is calling you),'* just the way the maid would sing.

'Late!' he added, making fun of me.

'Because of you,' I said getting up from the bed.

'Because of me?' He hunched up his shoulders.

'Who did not let me sleep when I should've? Well, I overslept because of that.'

'I see!' He made a face while I shouted to tell the maid that I would shortly be joining Mom in the puja room.

Our home was two adjacent flats on either side of the elevators. The building that we were a part of had two flats on every floor. This was unlike the rest of the buildings in the society with four flats per floor. Therefore the houses in our block were very spacious and people had their privacy. A year before marriage, Siddharth lived with his parents in one flat. But around the time of our engagement the family chose to buy the vacant flat next door. It was a wise decision given the expansion of the family as well as the family business.

Siddharth used the drawing room in our flat for his informal meetings. We used the living room in Mom and Dad's flat for all our family functions. The kitchen was common. It was where all the fresh vegetables from the family farmhouse would arrive every alternate day. It was where the Kaka—the very old family cook—would put into action his culinary skills following Mom's instructions. The entire family ate at the dining table in front of the kitchen in this flat. The common kitchen never let us feel that we lived in two different areas. Besides, most of the time the entrance doors of the two flats were left open.

'Nainaaaaaa . . . *aa jao, beta* . . .' Mom called out loud for me from the other flat.

'*Hanji, aai Mumaaa* . . .' I replied louder. I was late for the puja.

My day began in the other flat in the puja room. Not that I hated it, but I would've preferred a relaxed morning, sitting in the balcony sipping some tea. Mom and Dad did that. But then they got up quite early to be able to afford that time. There had been days when I would get up early and join them or carry my cup back to my bedroom and have it sitting next to Sid.

But today there was no time for tea. It was already seven. I took a quick shower and rushed into the puja room.

This was our ritual where apart from Sid, everybody in the house, including the maid and Kaka, would be present. The scion of the Singhania family had got a special excuse of golf. The game was a casual part of his formal work.

After puja while the maid and Kaka got busy in their chores, I sat with Mom and Dad to chit-chat. That's where I learnt of a bit of news that would be the biggest disappointment of my day.

'We will have to go to the farmhouse today,' Mom announced.

Upset, I recalled that it was the 15th of the month. On the 15th and 30th of every month, Mom and I visited the farmhouse. It was located at the outskirts of Gurgaon on the road towards Manesar. This is the place from where our kitchen sourced its vegetables. At times, milk as well. The caretaker and his family lived in the service quarter of our farmhouse. Every fifteen days, Mom and I would visit the place to monitor things. I had always enjoyed my stint in the garden where a variety of vegetables were planted, based on the season.

But I wasn't going to enjoy it any more. Not today, when I had been looking forward to going to the gym.

I was about to express my concern when Mom, noticing my disappointed face, asked me what the matter was.

I told her about my gym schedule and how a farmhouse visit would make me miss a session.

'You can miss it for one day,' she suggested without making too much of it.

I wish I had been more forceful in defending my schedule. But I wasn't. I made a mental note of either rescheduling my gym session on the 30th or the time of my visit.

Dad had just finished eating his share of *prasaad*. He asked, 'By the way, beta, how is your *gym-shym* going?'

I replied, 'It's going very well. I quite enjoy it.' A little ray of hope lit up a dark corner of my heart that was upset about missing gym. After all, somebody had finally asked me about what I had begun liking.

Then he looked at Mom and continued, 'Take your mom along as well. *Inka bhi kuch ho jayega* (She will also look better).' He was bantering with Mom who was literally double his size.

As the two of them got into yet another innocuous argument, I picked up my phone to type an SMS to Aarav.

'Won't be able to make it today. Sorry about this last-minute cancellation.'

In less than a minute the response came. 'Never mind.'

Seven

'Come on, three more to go . . . no . . . no . . . no . . . no . . . don't even think of giving up.'

It's been three weeks since I began the training. I liked the change in my appearance and daily routine.

However, physical training is not the only part of fitness. Even before he brings a noticeable change in your body, a trainer brings in visible changes in your kitchen.

I had already asked my cook to replace the refined oil we used with olive oil. The milkman from our farm had also been updated about my preference for low fat cow's milk so that he could add it to his morning supply list. And because the rest of the family only loved the taste of full cream buffalo milk, two kinds of milk were boiled in separate utensils on two different burners, often at the same time. The tasty cheese omelettes were a thing of the past. Boiled eggs were in, and their yolks flung out. Green tea sachets found their place on the tea counter. Almonds which my mother-in-law would give to her husband and her son became a part of my diet, as antioxidants, too.

The transformation did not stop at that. Sugar-free muesli and oats replaced parathas—just for me. To smell parathas in the morning and not eat them is quite an emotional hurdle to cross. So you inhale their aroma wafting out of the kitchen but you have to turn your face away and swallow your muesli instead! For the first time, I had begun to empathize with smokers and understood how difficult it must be for them to quit smoking.

Fitness discipline also brings in a change in your behaviour. In the retail stores, you now flip the packages of food products not just to see the MRP or expiry date, but also to read the nutritional value mentioned on them. I had started to scan the fat and carbohydrate percentages in all that I bought for the house. And then I realized that in the big food retail stores, there is very little that can be bought by a fitness freak. The chocolate and ice cream sections are of no use. Same is the case with the entire section storing chips, cookies and other assorted junk. The confectionary bay smells great, but all you can now pick from there is multigrain brown bread. Don't even look at the aisle with aerated and fruit drinks. They are all full of sugar. Basically, it is no fun visiting a retail store at all! You are better off at the neighbourhood *kirana* store. But then, they don't stock brown rice you see!

'Come on, ma'am! Let's finish this.'

More than the task of chalking out sets of exercises, the main task of a coach is to motivate you to push your boundaries so that you discover new limits. That's what Aarav was doing with me every day.

In merely three weeks, my stamina had increased. From thirty seconds I could hold a plank position for more than a minute now. I could run non-stop at 10 km per hour on the treadmill for straight ten minutes. I remember when I had begun, I would feel breathless in five minutes flat. The kettle-bell in my hands soon changed from 10 lbs to 15 lbs and I was confident I could lift 20 lbs as well.

I had lost a little more than 2.5 kg in the three weeks I had worked out. That was my achievement and the discovery thrilled me. However, according to Aarav, it was quite normal. He told me that fat loss in the initial few weeks is quite fast. But what I achieved beyond that was the real challenge. Nevertheless, my body felt toned and I felt more energetic and happier.

'Yes! Just two more left now. Come on, madam! Do it and feel proud!' he roared.

Aarav's way of motivating people was novel and interesting.

'Beyond this last repetition, there is glory waiting for you. Go claim it! It's yours!' he would cry out.

He would make me feel as if I was a gladiator!

He did this to me.

His words, and more importantly the energy with which he would deliver them, would have an enlivening influence on me. An influence I could rarely overcome. Hence, I seldom gave up.

And yet, there were those rare moments when I would cry, '*I can't! I can't!*' and feel like giving up. Aarav would bring his face closer to mine. And like a beast he would wildly look into my eyes and without blinking he would say, 'That's only in your mind. Tame your mind! And the body will follow. It will!'

His gaze and his words would penetrate my eyes and my mind. Somewhere deep inside me they would explode, generating enough energy for me to be able to ultimately finish my set. And that would mark my turning point.

Aarav had made the floor of the gym a battlefield for me. He made me claim my victory. In every fight!

Eventually, I got so used to all this that I ended up doing things which I never ever believed I could. It was one of the most important lessons I learnt from Aarav—*It's all in the mind*. Just the way he would say it, pointing his forefinger above his right ear.

After I would finish the set, he would raise his hand in the air. And I would respond. The two of us would do a high-five. We celebrated every successful completion of a set. That had become our ritual. It boosted my morale.

But then there were also moments when I was unwilling to give up, and Aarav intervened and stopped me. As an intelligent coach, he knew where to draw the line. If he saw an uncomfortable posture or shaky body balance, he would call it off.

'Dream big. But be practical. There's no point in wanting to become Amazing Spiderman when your town lacks tall buildings,' he had said in the first week of my training. He had stopped me from lifting a kettle-bell that was double the weight he had asked for. I thought I would impress him.

'What?' I had asked back. But he didn't answer and smilingly kept looking at my face to see if I got the meaning of his words.

'Wow! That was nice. Can you repeat that Spiderman line?' I insisted the moment I got it.

He ignored my compliment and said, 'I know you can do it, but I fear you will injure yourself.'

In subsequent weeks if anytime I would repeat this mistake he would remind me, 'Ma'am, the town still doesn't have tall buildings.'

Aarav meticulously maintained a track of my workouts. He kept a diary to monitor my progress. After every exercise, he would record the performance in terms of weight, repetitions or duration. The BMI report too was a part of this diary. That he did this for all his clients was impressive.

To look into his diary and see the changing graph of my abilities, within a span of three weeks, gave me a high. Slowly and steadily, I was undergoing a transition. Looking back at my little achievements in his diary, I imagined how many possibilities lay in front of me. I would look at the female fitness model posters mounted on the walls of the gym and I wanted to look as fabulous as them. Even though the Size-M goal was still a long way from where I stood three weeks on, it had begun to look more realistic than ever before.

For me, gym was not only about sweat and exercise. It meant a lot beyond. It had become a break from my stereotypical life at home. I would eagerly look forward to this time of the day. It was truly my time of the day and I derived a lot of satisfaction from it.

Spending time in the gym also meant a lot of fun for me. Manvika and I had an alternate day cardio-workout routine. On these days, Aarav did not train either of us. And quite often, if not always, the two of us exercised together and gossiped a lot; more so when we were in the steam room twice a week. The juice counter, the ladies' room, the steam room—the gym had become our space to hold long girly heart-to-heart conversations.

On other days, Aarav trained Manvika at 10 a.m. for about an hour, followed by training me at 11.30 a.m. The three of us would often sit together and chit-chat at the juice counter between 11 and 11.30. I remember the first day all of us got together, how Manvika was shocked when she found out that the guy whose car I ran my car into was Aarav. She kept interrogating Aarav on why he didn't shout at me.

This chatting around at the juice space had been Manvika's routine for a long time in that gym. I was the new entrant to this hangout. I would arrive half an hour before my session especially to catch up with Manvika. During our chats Manvika would drink her protein shake and I would eat a banana or a sandwich as my pre-workout meal. The juice bay was also the place to check in our cellphones. Aarav did not allow any of us to carry our cellphones during the workout.

'Ma'am, you will have to keep this back in the locker,' he had said on the first day of our training session, just when I had started to stretch.

'But why?' I had asked with great disappointment. I remember his exact response.

'A) It's a distraction. You won't be able to focus on your exercises. B) The random calls interfere and end up extending the gap between consecutive sets. C) It's uncomfortable to work out carrying it in your pocket. It will certainly interfere with a few exercises. D) Which means you will keep it somewhere on the floor, but then you don't want to see a random weight falling down on your phone. That happens quite often in this gym. And I don't wish that you learn it the hard way. E) Besides, someone can steal your phone while you are busy working out. And let me tell you that I personally don't care about D and E.'

I had laughed deliberating how he was only concerned about the reasons that affected his coaching.

So, in the gym, cellphones were checked only at the juice bay. On training days, I hung out at the juice counter twice. The second time it would be after the workout, in Aarav's company. Manvika would have long left. And this would be my time to have my whey protein.

Often, during our post-workout chit-chats, Aarav and I would talk about our day-to-day lives. At times, he would share an interesting event that had transpired in the gym. If nothing else, a mere look at the TV stations in front of the series of treadmills would bring up some current or political event to talk about. But what I really enjoyed the most during these talks was the fact that this was when Aarav would transform from being a strict professional coach into a friend who would crack jokes and make me laugh.

Our post-workout talks on Mondays would be the best. Sunday being a holiday would provide us a long break from each other, so there would be a lot to talk about. Like, the new restaurants we'd tried out over the weekend or the movies we'd watched.

In the beginning of the second week, I had discovered a peculiar thing about Aarav. My personal trainer, who instructed what I should eat and what I shouldn't, and often forbade me from touching my favourite dishes, was himself a big foodie. He followed this concept of a cheat-meal day; something he suggested to all his clients, including me.

'Once a week you can eat whatever you want to. But in a limited quantity!' he had told me one Monday afternoon after finishing the workout.

I had expressed shock when he told me that he loved mango ice cream and had had it for dessert the day before. I had called him a hypocrite.

But then he clarified, 'Pick a day. I would say choose a weekend, as that's when we usually go out to eat or go shopping and pick up something to eat. Make it a cheat-meal day.'

This guy makes everything so interesting. Claim your glory! Cheat-meal day!

'Cheat-meal day! How exciting it sounds!' I had reacted.

And as I said that, I recalled our diet-plan discussion that took place on the first day of our training. I had already expressed my love for food, from the extravagantly luscious choco-lava cake to the mouthwatering *aaloo-tikki*. Even though I knew I had to distance myself from all such guilty pleasures, I thought giving up white rice and replacing it with a salad was too much to ask for.

'I hate lettuce leaves, zucchini, broccoli, mushrooms, olives and all that kind of stuff. It's all raw and tasteless!' I had said making a face.

'You decide whether you want to eat what's right for your body or what's right for your taste buds.' Back then Aarav had left it up to me.

And precisely at that moment, I had formed Aarav's image in my mind as someone who only ate healthy food and would hate me if I didn't follow the same.

'You don't even have a little love for food. You won't understand what I am saying,' I'd said, disappointed.

My statement had hurt him. In the debate that had followed, the only argument I had was that he wouldn't understand my cravings for food. To which he had asked me to list all the things I craved for. The items were in double digits. Aarav's response to it had left me amazed. He had got his mobile phone and showed me a photo of him from the past. I could not believe my eyes when I saw the really fat guy who looked like him.

'This is me, madam!'

He must have been some 100-plus kg!

'I craved for and ate everything that you have on your list. In fact, a lot more. Even today I crave for so many things. And therefore I need determination to overcome such temptations. A lack of love for food would never demand determination. Just because I can stop myself doesn't mean I don't want them.'

In that moment, I had seen a self-disciplined person in Aarav. And also, on seeing his transition from the overweight person in the picture to the fit one standing in front of me, I was not left with any other choice but to follow a disciplined diet.

'Ma'am, if you want to meet your goal, you will have to give all this food up, and follow a lean diet.' He had made it clear.

I recalled how disappointed I had looked because I knew there was *kadhi-chawal* with deep fried *pakoday* at home for lunch that day.

'All right! Fine!' I had said with a heavy heart.

Exactly three weeks after this discussion, I discovered that the foodie in him had not completely died. That the cheat-meal day was his window to eat anything that he wanted, but not beyond a certain calorific limit. For example, if he had a *naan* at dinner he'd make sure it wasn't a butter naan. He would either have a sweet or a scoop of ice cream for dessert but not both. If he ate a burger or a pizza, given its high calorie count, he wouldn't have anything from the forbidden list for the rest of the day.

'Workout and diet plans should not make you feel deprived of the little pleasures of life,' he had said while explaining the rationale behind his cheat-meal day. I quite enjoyed his reasoning and the fact that I too could have a cheat-meal day.

I also liked the idea of a cheat-meal day because it sounded forbidden—and therefore, adventurous.

How the two of us looked forward to our weekend cheat-meal day! And then to the next day when we told each other about our respective cheating. It had become a Monday ritual for us.

My in-laws had discussed my diet plan with Siddharth over dinner. It had been embarrassing. Thankfully, Sid had supported me and said it was up to me to decide what I wanted to eat. I was happy for a moment. Then he said that he was happy I was trying to look good.

Look good? Wasn't I already pretty? Why did my beauty have to depend on my weight? Yet I kept quiet and didn't say a thing. Everyone continued to eat as if they had done me a favour by trying to be understanding.

Eight

I continued to hurt till we had the fight.

'It's been more than four months, Sid, since we visited my family in Delhi.'

'But you only went last month,' he argued back.

'I said *we* Siddharth!'

'Oho! What difference will my presence make? What will I do there?'

'What do you do when you meet your fellow builders and investors and clients and bureaucrats?' I asked.

'I discuss business with them, Naina,' he replied.

'So now, in order to meet you my family will have to invest in your projects. Buy your property!' I was going on a different tangent. I knew he didn't mean this at all. But I had been frustrated with Siddharth's lack of attention towards me. And I didn't want him to totally ignore my blood relations. A visit to my family once in two months was all I had asked for.

'Is that what you think?' Sid asked throwing his hands up in the air as a sign of frustration.

It took me a moment to realize that I might have gone too far. 'I am sorry,' I said but made it clear that my apology didn't change my accusation by turning my back towards him.

'Naina . . .' Sid softened his voice and held my shoulders from behind. 'I get bored.'

'At my place?' I verified without turning my head towards him.

He didn't say anything but nodded in the mirror in front of us.

'What if I say the same? And I live here,' I said. That I was hurt showed in my eyes and the tears that flowed.

Sid didn't have an answer. I didn't wait for him to respond either. I didn't want him to see my tears. I felt a distance between us—like I couldn't say what I wanted to, like I was supposed to keep quiet and take it, like I was the guest in this house.

I went to pack my gym bag and left early, even before Sid had stepped out for his office. I planned to visit a salon first and then head for the gym.

~

I caught Aarav on the treadmill. In his light grey vest and gym shorts, he was busy doing his warm-up jog. My mood brightened immediately. I put aside my negative thoughts from my fight with Sid. There was an unoccupied treadmill next to his. I walked fast to grab it, lest someone else took it first. Treadmills are the busiest machines in any gym.

'Hi!' I said adjusting my sipper on the dashboard panel ahead of me.

'Oh, hello!' Aarav said looking at me. I immediately felt warm and secure with him.

'We are working out together, right?' I reminded him.

'Of course we are! Seven minutes of warm-up and then stretch,' he advised me.

'Yup!' I said as I pressed the speed button on the mill and began my brisk walking. I was glad I had things to do when all was not okay at home. I thought about how nice it was with Aarav by my side and us exercising together. So what if—

And then there was an awkward moment. In my hurry to grab the treadmill I hadn't even noticed the LCD panel above me. This one was tuned into FTV, Fashion TV! In this gym, no TV repeated any other channel—they were all on a diverse range of channels. In spite of the option of being able to change channels, no one on the treadmills ever bothered to tinker with them. I never saw anyone plugging in the earphones attached to the arm of their treadmills either. They all simply watched the screen. Besides, the news and business channels anyway ran the breaking news marquee and the English movie channels showed subtitles.

The LCD above my treadmill was designated for FTV. I had so far always avoided taking this treadmill. Even though many members didn't have any issue with it, certain shows on this channel made me uncomfortable when I watched with everyone around. But then today, in a hurry, I had made my choice.

A model in a satin bikini was rolling over in the wet sand on the sea beach. She was surrounded by a crew that held the light reflectors. Right beside her stood the make-up artist. The fashion photographer shot her in various seductive poses. At one point the photographer rushed to her and adjusted the strap of her bra. From over her right collarbone he had pulled it down on to her shoulder. Embarrassed by the scene, I shifted my eyes from the LCD to the dashboard panel of my treadmill. *Oh god, I have to pretend I wasn't watching any of it!* The world behind me would be watching me watch this photoshoot of almost naked women posing away! I was petrified at that thought. My eyes were glued to the changing timer on the treadmill panel. I wanted the power to go off.

At that instant, all I wanted was not to look at the LCD screen. And I ended up doing the exact opposite. It is just like when you are asked not to think of elephants for the next one minute all you do is think about elephants. The more I tried not to look at the screen, the more I did. Has the photoshoot ended? Is there an ad break that has momentarily halted the demonstration of a lingerie model soaked in seawater and smeared in sand? How is she managing to look so ruggedly sexy?

Hoooh! What am I doing? Why am I not able to keep my eyes on the dashboard?

And then I thought I would talk with Aarav, so that I could keep my mind off the goddamn TV! The moment I turned my head towards him, I was taken aback. Aarav's eyes were glued on the panel in front of me and he was watching the FTV shoot. On my LCD screen! Without any guilt! I quickly shifted my eyes back on to the dashboard of my treadmill.

God! Men!

For some reason, the idea of Aarav watching that photoshoot, on the TV screen on my side, bothered me. On the dark glass panel wall in front of me, behind which a series of these LCDs were installed, I sneaked a look at the shadowy mirror image of Aarav. Indeed his head was tilted towards the screen in front of me. From the corner of my eye I then looked at Aarav's TV screen. The news channel on it had run into an ad break. There was an image of Aarav I had in my mind. I chose to safely believe that it was only due to the ad break that he had shifted his attention on to my screen.

But I was wrong. About three minutes of brisk walking was left. The news was back on Aarav's screen but his eyes were still on my screen.

Something in me wanted Aarav not to spoil my image of him. Perhaps, not for his sake. But for my own. I didn't want to step down to change the channel. I didn't want to step down to move to a different treadmill either. All of it would have made my discomfort obvious. That's why I thought about interfering.

I made up my mind to confront Aarav. Of all the people, I couldn't tolerate *him* as this person who wasn't sensitive enough about my presence and thereby my discomfort.

'Aarav!' I said a bit sharply.

He shifted his gaze from the TV panel to me as he said, 'Yes?'

'What is so interesting about this channel?' I indicated at the screen in front of me. I couldn't believe I had just said that.

Aarav looked at me agape, trying to find out what I meant. And then for a moment he looked back at that almost naked model draped in wet sand, the froth-laden salty waves washing the sand off her body. And then he hit his forehead with the palm of his hand. The next moment he looked at me, he was smiling and shaking his head in disbelief. He had whispered the word, 'Unbelievable!'

I wanted him to say something more. To react to it, to talk to me. But he chose to dismiss the idea. He smiled, shifted his focus back on the dashboard of his machine and increased the speed.

'Last one minute of warm-up left!' he announced as he picked up his speed.

His reaction bothered me enough to increase my speed even though I wasn't supposed to. So, I sprinted too. My meaningless action meant something to me. By now I had forgotten Sid.

Our argument had shifted further back into the mind. I was thinking of Aarav who had turned his head to take note of my speed and yet chose not to say anything. In that one minute of sprinting, I was not only demonstrating against Aarav's dismissal of my question but also wondering if somewhere I had ended up showcasing my conservative mindset in a liberal, high tech gym. And if I was unreasonably insecure about something? Whatever it was, I tried to forget it as soon as I stepped off the treadmill and went to stretch my muscles.

Aarav brought a pair of kettle-bells of different weights and a bosu ball.

'Ma'am, today we will do HIIT—' Aarav had only begun when I cut him short.

'—HIIT?' I asked.

'High intensity interval training. We will do a circuit of four exercises with only the transitional break involved. After finishing the fourth exercise we will take a break. We will do three such circuits. Okay?'

'Okay,' I said retying my hair into a ponytail as my head was soaking wet in sweat.

He then named the exercises. Fifteen reps of the kettle-bell swing, twenty slams of the battle rope, twenty each-leg mountain-climb on the bosu ball and finally fifteen each-side wood chop on the resistance tube.

One benefit of professional training is that you get to know the names of the exercises. Something I did not have any idea about before.

'So do we do this together? Like at the same time?' I checked.

'Yes, now here's the fun part,' Aarav began.

I wanted to know how he was going to make it an interesting session—just like any other day!

'We will do this as a team. Okay?'

I had a fair idea but I waited for details. I looked at his face as he spoke. I watched his body language. How excited his face had become, how much concentration reflected in his eyes!

'This equipment . . . the bosu . . . the resistance tube . . . these kettle-bells . . . all of them belong to our opponent team.' I wondered if I'd heard him right and paid extra attention.

This is not the time to concentrate on him. Think about the task! I scolded myself.

'To finish the circuit in a defined time is our mission. If we give up in the middle or finish it beyond the defined time, we will lose to their team. You get that?'

This guy could literally turn non-living entities into living beings. And make them belong to a team. And make humans compete with them!

He continued to speak. 'We will do this alternately. First you will finish the four exercises and the moment you are done I will start.'

Just like every other day, my coach had made the workout pretty adventurous and exciting for me. And today I was in his team. For the first time we were going to work out together. I wanted to make him proud. He had charged my adrenaline and I was all motivated to give my 100 per cent.

But I had a thought. 'Is it fair that you and I have the same goals?' I asked smiling.

He looked at me. Then said, 'No!' Then he pointed to a 40 lb kettle-bell. 'That's my kettle-bell.' I compared it to mine. Mine was 20 lb. It cleared the picture.

'Besides, my goals on the bosu, heavy rope and resistance tube are also double that of yours. You must count when I do, for I will count yours,' he said with a smile on his face.

It's one thing to get trained by a trainer. It's another to be in his team. More so, when it's just you and him in the team. *It's a day to prove and be worthy of the faith your trainer has put in you.* I was full of gratitude. I wanted to keep up his faith in me.

Coincidental as it was, just when we were about to begin, the soundtrack changed. And to our delight it was the Jean Cena theme track—Aarav's favourite! He had told me about this in the initial days of our training. 'I can lift this entire stack of weight listening to this track,' he had said making me do a pulley pushdown the moment the song began.

'Oh! It's my favourite number.' I could see it in his eyes.

'Yes I know. Remember you told me?'

He smiled and nodded.

'Leverage the power of music to motivate yourself,' he would often say. 'Leverage your anger, if any—learn to channelize it in your exercise. Leverage the mirrors in the gym to look at yourself and see a better you in it.' He also told me that he wore vests, instead of T-shirts, during his workout, so that he could see a lot of his muscles in the mirror. 'Self-motivation,' he said. I agreed with him. After all, he looked his super best in his vests, revealing his traps muscles over his collarbone and rock-like shoulders.

On that particular day, he added something else to this list of leveraging things from one's surroundings.

'Leverage the glimpse of an attractive body of an FTV model. Not every look is suggestive. Admire the attractiveness of a well-maintained body. Derive motivation, if you can,' he said and reclaimed his previous image in my mind. He didn't offend me but very subtly conveyed his point. Yet, I felt embarrassed of my old-school perspective about certain things.

Even though, initially, I wasn't a big fan of all the English tracks that were played in the gym, over a period of time, I had started liking them. It was the only time of the day I was in the midst of loud and peppy music that boosted everyone's morale. At one point I got so used to the gym's playlist that as soon as one track ended, my mind knew the next one by default. Aarav or I, and at times both of us, would sing the tune before it began. We were right most of the times!

'That's ten. Keep going . . .'

Just like any other day, Aarav kept boosting my morale. I was giving my best. I had a role to play in *our* victory against the imaginary opponents.

'Butts up . . . butts up . . . ma'am . . . you are falling down.'

I struggled to lift my body and finish the last few mountain climbs. My speed dropped with every subsequent climb. Yet, I focused on lifting my behind and pulling my knees up to touch my elbows with all my strength. At one point, I felt my arms didn't have the strength to hold my body and that any moment I would fall.

'Keep up the pace, ma'am; just five more to go. Giving up is not a choice. Not when you are this close.'

I went for another one.

'That's nice. Open your mouth and breathe. Open your mouth, ma'am.'

I inhaled and exhaled from the mouth as I made another climb. Just then my arms fumbled and I struggled to hold myself from falling.

'Recall your mission. Die! But don't surrender. And should you have to die, then I say die beyond the finish line,' he roared like my commander in a war.

His words fuelled me with aggression. And I don't know how, but I landed up quickly finishing my set and dropped my body on the floor in order to relax. By the end of the first circuit, my face and my top were drenched in sweat. My heartbeats had gone up. I was panting heavily. I continued to breathe in and breathe out from my mouth. When Aarav extended his hand for a high-five, I could not even lift my arm!

I just smiled a satisfied smile. A smile of having achieved something and making Aarav proud.

He brought his palm down, closer to my hand. With his other hand he opened my palm and then high-fived.

That was so damn cute!

That tap was as if I had passed on the baton to Aarav to finish the pending race. It was his turn now. As I watched him perform the circuit, I pulled myself up and walked to get my sipper. He effortlessly finished the first set and moved to the next exercise. I focused on his posture and his temperament. I derived motivation from him. I wanted to perform the way he performed. I noticed his chiselled body, full of muscle, without any fat, as it began to glow with sweat under the white gym lights.

'You've got to boost me up too. I need motivation!' he demanded the moment his favourite song ended.

I could clearly see he didn't need any motivation and he was good without it. But by asking me for it he reminded me that he wasn't my coach at that moment, but my team mate. Yet the thought of boosting his morale tickled me.

'Come on, boy! Five more to go,' I roared imitating Aarav at the same time trying to control my laugh.

It was funny that I was calling a guy my age 'boy', while he would call me madam. But, hell, I enjoyed calling him this way!

I noticed his posture when he was doing the mountain climb. Precisely, his 'butts'. How easily he had referred to my 'butts'! I smiled. It was easy to say all this in the gym.

As I watched Aarav's butts I realized he too would have watched mine! I bit my lower lip. I suddenly shouted, 'Butts up, Aarav . . . butts up!'

He looked at the side mirror to verify his posture as he continued with his reps.

'Ma'am . . . huh . . . the law of gravity . . . huh . . . would not allow . . . huh . . . me to take my butts up any more . . . huh,' he said gasping for breath.

I burst into laughter.

When Aarav finished his circuit, for the first time, I became the first one to initiate a high-five. One battle was won. There were two more to go. We took a break before we kick-started the second round. It turned out to be even more difficult than the first.

The moment I finished round two, my heartbeats were racing so fast that I could feel the thud it my chest without even placing my hand over it. It was shaking my entire body. And then suddenly I felt weak and sleepy.

I told Aarav. 'Am I going to faint? I guess I am.' Worried, I checked as I stopped walking and held on to the machine.

'Did you eat well this morning?' he asked.

I nodded.

'Don't worry then. Nothing will happen. It's the shortage of oxygen supply to the brain. Your body is burning oxygen three times faster than otherwise. That's the reason you are breathing through your mouth to inhale more oxygen and release more carbon dioxide from your body.'

Seconds later, I realized I'd survived and didn't faint. But then something strange happened in that moment. I pressed both my ears, first with my fingers and then with my palms. Worried, I looked at Aarav. But even before I could explain he smiled looking at me and asked back, *'Kaan band ho rahe hain* (Your ears are blocked)?'

I didn't hear him clearly, but read his lips. The music and the hum in the gym had all fallen down by many decibel levels in my ears. It was like being on the plane while landing and take-off.

That he knew what I was going through offered some relief. 'How do you know?' I could barely hear my own voice.

He came close and shouted to make himself heard, 'Often happens during HIIT. Don't worry, this too isn't life threatening. Just that it's uncomfortable.'

I continued to struggle with my ears, trying to unblock them.

At one moment without announcing he held my face steady in this hands. I was surprised but I didn't resist. He then pinched my nostrils, thereby blocking out air flow. 'Ma'am, try to blow air out without opening your mouth. Let the air pass with a rush into your eardrums.'

I let him hold my nose as I carefully followed the steps. I didn't want to sneeze over his hands. 'Harder!' he shouted when he witnessed my miserable attempt. In my third attempt, with a sudden pop, my ears went back to normal. It was such a relief.

'But why did it happen?' I asked.

'Incorrect breathing! Perhaps, you were inhaling fast with your mouth but only relying on your nose to exhale. Or perhaps after deep inhalations you were holding your breath. In such scenarios, you see, the air can't escape. It flows backwards into the ear tubes where it gets trapped. The ears respond to these trapped air pockets by popping up.'

'You are a genius!' I said patting my trainer's broad shoulders.

He grinned, 'That I am, madam.'

'Can I request something from you?'

'Sure!'

'Can you please stop calling me madam?'

'Aa . . . sure . . . I can try.'

'Cool,' I said smiling.

Later that day, after the workout, in the shower of the gym, I recalled how Aarav had rescued me from my discomfort. How, first he'd held my face in between his palms in order to make me still. Under the running shower, I imitated his action of pressing my nostrils in between his thumb and forefinger. The next instant I was laughing at my stupidity, splashing the water falling over me, up in the air, back at the showerhead.

Nine

Ping!

That was my phone

'Howz the cheat-meal day going?'

Aarav's WhatsApp message interrupted my reading one Sunday noon.

I was pleasantly surprised. In the past four months, his only reason to text me was to confirm my schedule for the next day.

It was a practice most of the trainers in the gym followed. Every evening they texted their clients, asking them whether or not they planned to attend their sessions scheduled for the subsequent day. On a weekly average, at least 25 per cent of the planned sessions would get cancelled. Sometimes it was work pressure, at other times personal chores, and if nothing else, simply a change in mood, resulted in cancellations. Reaching out to their clients a day before helped the trainers plan their work better. And yet there were the last-minute dropouts or calls seeking time change.

But he had never reached out to me like this before. Not Aarav. Not on a Sunday afternoon, which was our off day. Even though the subject matter was professional, there was a casual feel to it. That made it casually professional!

This message was a refreshing change from his routine copy-pasted one liner *Please-confirm-the-session-tomorrow* in the history of my WhatsApp chat window. And that initiated a change in my response. Instead of the regular 'Yes' and the rare 'No', this time I replied, 'Had *paneer ke pranthey* for breakfast ☺'

The emoticon reflected the smile on my face as I sent that reply.

'And what's for lunch?' He came back rather quickly with his next question.

Usually, this would make for our Monday after-workout discussion. For some strange reason, Aarav chose to have it on WhatsApp. I was happy to write back, '*Rajma chaawal!* It's brown rice. So it's not a cheat-meal.'

'That's nice,' he wrote back.

I chose yet another smiley face and sent him as an acknowledgement of his comment. And just then the grey ticks beneath them turned blue.

I thought he would write something again in reply. I wanted him to do that.

But he didn't. Not for a couple of seconds after which his online status vanished. That's the thing with sending a smiley face. While it fills the void when you don't have anything to say, it also marks the end of the conversation.

I wanted to write back to Aarav. Something! Anything! But I don't know why I didn't. I guess I didn't know what to write. I dropped my phone on the bed and resumed my reading.

I read a paragraph or two, but for some reason, I could not focus well. I was curious to check my phone again. And so I did, even though there was no new notification.

Aarav's status appeared: *Online*. Again! Not that I was sad a moment ago, but his available status made me happy. And I became happier when my phone showed he was typing again.

This simple status—*typing . . .*—felt nice to even look at. There is so much hope embedded in it. I realized how much mystery there is in someone *typing . . .* Of course, it depends on the person you are in conversation with. It sets an anticipation—some sort of curiosity that leaves you joyfully impatient. This definite knowledge that the other person wants to have a conversation with you, that he has you in mind, and that soon you will get to know it. Soon! I don't know why I thought of all this while I was staring at my phone.

Strangely, the next moment from *typing . . .* he went back to simply being online.

He too would have seen me online—I realized. And wondered—*Should I type something?*

Once again, I saw him typing, and then he again second-guessed himself. It was weird. Aarav had never behaved this way earlier. I could sense that he wanted to talk, but could not figure out what exactly to talk about or perhaps the best words to phrase what he wanted to say. But then, unlike me, at least he was making an effort!

He was again typing something.

But this time I could not hold myself back. Before he could change his mind, I ended up writing very quickly, 'Not sure about dinner yet!'

Just then his message arrived, 'What are you doing right now?' He had sent the message at the same time as me!

'Oh! You can afford to have a small dessert after dinner,' he responded to the message I had sent him.

But then I hadn't responded to his.

I wondered how to react to this new way in which Aarav was reaching out to me. *Since when did he get interested to know what I was doing at a particular point in a day?*

At the same time, I wondered why I was getting conscious about it. After all, this is how we talked to each other at the gym. But this was the first time he wanted to have a conversation with me beyond the gym timings, in the privacy of WhatsApp chat. *Is there anything wrong in what he had asked? No . . . Not at all! I wonder why we had never had phone chats before!*

'Reading a book.'

'What's it about?'

'It's a love story,' I wrote back, even though I was actually reading a crime thriller. It was a deliberate provocation.

'Okay,' he wrote back.

I thought he could have written a longer response. 'Do you read?' I asked him.

'Nothing beyond the science of bodybuilding ☺' he answered and then, 'At times the newspaper.'

'Ha ha! Well, if you are not reading books, you are missing something incredible in your life.'

'Hmm . . .' he wrote back.

Just like that single smiley emoticon, this 'hmm' also indicates the end of a conversation. But he hadn't initiated the conversation to end it this way. Neither did I want it to.

'I like this book that I am reading.'

'Good for you!'

Damn it! Ask me something about the love story I said I was reading!

He sent the next text—'Here I am getting bored ☹'

I imagined his sad face.

'Why so? Where are you?'

'At the gym. A couple of rescheduled sessions got cancelled after I reached the gym. Nothing to do!'

'Well, go home, then.'

'I don't have a family at home. It's boring out there as well. Besides, I have to collect supplements from a delivery boy who will come here in an hour or so.'

Aarav's family was in Gwalior and he lived in a rented apartment in Gurgaon. This I knew. I also knew that he shared it with another personal trainer from the same gym. He had told me this long back.

I was about to type something, but at the last minute I changed my ploy. 'Call Manvika to the gym. She's usually free on Sunday afternoons.'

'Of course, when you are busy enjoying reading . . .'

There, he'd got an opportunity!

'What do you mean?' I asked. *Why was he being sarcastic?*

'I would have enjoyed your company more than Manvika's.' He was even more direct than I was!

This isn't the Aarav who was training me! Since when did he start feeling that he needs me? Today, when he has nothing else to do? Or is he lying, just the way I had lied about the genre of the book I had been reading?

That he needed my company was a joyful realization. That he said it in so many words made me even happier.

There was this strange excitement within me. Siddharth was busy playing golf with his friends and then he had a lunch thing planned with them as well. Given that I wasn't doing much and that I only had to cross the road in front of my building to be at the gym and see Aarav, made this unplanned meeting easy and exciting.

'I am not that busy reading . . .' I tried to subtly change my position.

'Then come down,' Aarav wrote.

'Give me 15 mins.'

I felt genuinely nice when I confirmed that I would be meeting him. There was some kind of thrill to it that I had not experienced for many years in my life. I had been crossing the road in front of my society every day to go to the gym. But that day it felt different. It felt like I was breaking the rules. It felt fulfilling. More so, because the person at the other end had reached out.

Also because he'd shown he needed me.

'Sure.'

Ten

In a short while I was with Aarav. We sat at our usual place—the juice counter. It was a perfect place to catch up. It didn't make us conspicuous. Our meetings got camouflaged as work related. Even though they were not. Not this time, at least.

The music was playing in the background, just like any other day. But there were very few people in the gym. Aarav placed an order for two blueberry walnut smoothies. I sat back with several thoughts in my mind; at the same time I wanted to know what was running in Aarav's mind. *Why did he suddenly want to be close to me?*

'Cheers!' he said raising the long smoothie glass.

We smiled at each other, tinkled the glasses and savoured the taste of the rich thick purple smoothie. It was my favourite. Aarav knew this. He had ordered it without even asking me. It felt nice that I had someone who knew me well and cared enough for what I liked. I recalled how Siddharth always wanted me to do what he liked; I could do what I liked only in my own time.

'So?' he said as soon as he took a big sip.

'So?' I raised my eyebrows.

He didn't like my look and asked, 'Why are you making this face?'

'Nothing,' I said lightly.

'But still?' he insisted.

So I asked, 'All's okay with you?'

'And why do you feel that it's not?'

'Because till date, you've never asked me to join you.' I paused for a second and added, 'Not when I am not in the gym.'

I knew I was putting him in a spot. But I enjoyed doing that.

Aarav kept looking into my eyes.

'Did I trouble you by asking you to come here?' he enquired.

'No,' I said staring back into his eyes as the smoothie slid down the back of my throat.

And then after a moment of thoughtful silence at the other end, Aarav spoke, 'Even I was wondering about this.'

'Wondering about what, Aarav?'

'Why did I call you? I have never called any of my clients ever,' he confessed innocently.

I looked at his face and could sense that he had more to add. He didn't need me to fill the gaps with my questions. I chose to remain quiet. I felt it was the right thing to do.

He looked away from me, somewhere into the depth of his smoothie and said, 'I felt like . . . like . . . I needed your company. So I asked for it.'

Then he looked back at me, his eyes boring into mine. I couldn't say a thing. My heart was beating fast. I could almost hear it.

'Initially, I was hesitant about asking you . . .' With the innocence of a schoolboy, he'd charmingly admitted to everything.

'I could sense that . . .' I said.

'You did?'

'You kept deleting and rewriting those messages. I could see that and make out,' I said.

A hesitant smile appeared on his face and then vanished in a split second. He looked like he was thinking about something.

'You must have found that awkward?'

'I did.'

But I didn't want him to overthink it so I also said, 'But I liked that you reached out to me. You could have called anyone. So chill!'

That boosted his spirits. His face relaxed.

'I wouldn't have reached out to anyone else,' he said with a confident smile.

I laughed. 'Why?'

'Hmm . . . I don't know.' He shrugged his broad shoulders. 'I guess I find you more interesting than others,' he chuckled.

'Aarav! Are you flirting with me?'

He shook his head. His mouth was full of smoothie he had just sipped. We both laughed. *Wasn't this flirting?*

'If being honest is what you call flirting then . . .'

'Hmm . . .' I pretended to think.

'It takes guts for a man to be this honest. I mean, this openly honest,' he added.

I thought I was trying to take a dig at Aarav, put him in a spot. But the conversation was now taking a different turn. It was attaining seriousness, but in a candid sort of way. It was beautiful and funny and refreshing!

'Hmm . . . all right! I will take your words on face value,' I said. I was feeling light and happy and something inside me wanted this never to end.

His eyes were still on me. There was something deep in them. *Why couldn't I just look away?*

'By the way, if you had a girlfriend, you would have impressed her with this statement.'

'Did I?'

'What?'

'Impress you?'

'I said girlfriend, Aarav!'

'But you did . . . a bit,' I said with a smile. It was fun teasing him as he took everything I said seriously. I watched him as he again seemed to slip into thinking mode.

'Why don't you have a girlfriend?' I asked interrupting his thoughts.

I knew that was quite direct. But I also knew that I could afford to be this straightforward with him.

'Should I have one?'

'Of course.'

'And what makes you think that?'

'You are a good human being! A gentleman! Handsome! Fit and attractive! I am sure a lot of women would be interested in you.'

The praise didn't move him even a bit. There wasn't any noticeable change on his face.

'I had one when I was in college,' he recalled and said.

'What happened then?'

'She broke up.'

'Why?'

'She wanted to be with someone who aspired for a 9 to 5 white-collar corporate job. I was more interested in fitness as my career. For her my job was that of keeping used dumb-bells back in the rack. "We are not fit for each other," she said. She moved on. I moved on.'

'Was it difficult to move on?'

'Initially, yes! But later, I changed the way I looked at it. It helped.'

'What way was that, Aarav?'

'Oh that! Well, I realized that a break-up isn't the end of the world. I am not the only one dealing with it. Billions have had a break-up. Trillions are yet to have it. I had a life before she moved into it. Now that she is gone, all I need to do is go find that life back.'

I couldn't help but to clap on Aarav's way to motivate himself after the break-up. No wonder he motivates so many of his clients on the floor of the gym. For a few seconds none of us talked. I was absorbing his perspective.

Then I asked him, 'But what about now? I am sure lot of females here in the gym would be interested in you.'

'It is also important that I should be interested in them,' he said and looked at me. He didn't appear arrogant. He was not. He was just being honest.

Referring to his colleagues, he mentioned, 'On weekends, my friends regularly visit the high-end clubs here in Gurgaon. In those late night parties, single women do show interest in them just because of their attractive physique. They know it and therefore they wear skin-fit T-shirts.' He laughed.

'You don't go with them?'

'Sometimes!'

'And the idea of dancing with those pretty single women doesn't excite you?'

He smiled. A momentary shyness twinkled in his eyes. And he looked here and there before resuming eye contact.

'Aaaa . . . not the unknown ones. Not when they are so drunk that they won't even remember my name once they are out of their hangover the next afternoon.'

'Hmm . . . I see! So what kind of woman would interest you?'

'Your kind.'

I caught my breath. *Had he just said that?*

I'd heard it clearly. He had said that. There wasn't a minute's hesitation in Aarav when he said that. He meant it.

In a single second he stole away all my thoughts from me. I didn't know how to react. I shifted my eyes to the glass in my hand, in spite of the fact it was empty by then. How do I react when I myself didn't know how exactly I felt? I couldn't make out whether it was something to worry about or whether it was meant as a compliment. Or the truth was probably in-between.

Should I be bothered about it or should I be happy about it? This definitely can't be both. That I was unable to decide was in fact my first worry.

Our chat had ventured into a dangerous territory. We could both sense that. The only problem was that neither of us wanted to back out of this conversation. It was getting addictive.

He didn't point to me exactly. He said my kind. He meant like me. Not me. But then the challenging part was—what should be my response?

So I looked at him and ended up stating the obvious. 'I'll take that as a compliment.' I smiled.

Aarav nodded his head slightly. Certain despair loomed in between the lines on his forehead. I sensed that since he was quiet. He shifted his gaze to the glass in my hand.

'And if I may ask, what exactly do you like about my kind?' I said to take the conversation forward.

He smiled only a bit at the glass. The next moment he looked at me with seriousness again. *What had gotten into him today?*

'Everything about you, Naina.'

Naina . . . He'd made it sound sensuous! Aarav seldom called me by my name. Never in this way! Never this direct! Never in this proximity! Ever since I had insisted he call me by my name instead of madam, I had not heard him use it too often, unless he was calling me from a distance or referring to me while talking to Manvika.

'. . . I mean your kind,' he corrected himself abruptly. But the damage was already done.

I secretly enjoyed his mistake and continued with my questions, 'All right, point taken. And how do you define my kind?'

'I may not be able to define the entire kind, as I have rarely come across someone like you, but I can tell you what I admire in you.'

There was no way I would not love what he was going to say, 'Which is?'

'Your simplicity. There's an innocence in you, which is so attractive and rare these days. The grace with which you carry yourself doesn't come across as attitude.'

'That's it?' I laughed. 'What more?'

'Hmm . . . you are not pretentious, you are not insecure, you don't throw tantrums, you don't bitch about people behind their backs . . . all these are such common traits in most of the women in this gym, and also men I would say. You are a genuinely good human being at heart. And of course, you are beautiful!'

That afternoon, Aarav opened up to me like never before. At times, he paused to frame his thoughts, to find the right words. I looked at the black in his eyes; how they frequently moved. I observed his facial expressions; the little smile that played hide-and-seek on his lips. How, at times, in his attempt to find the right words he unconsciously ran his hand through his hair—which on other days was under his cap. At times, I manoeuvred the conversation in such a way that it enabled him the opportunity to speak. I wasn't sure if he needed me. I guessed it was I who needed him. He was honest in being upfront about everything he felt for me. Yet, he didn't cross the line. He admired me, but he didn't say he was attracted to me. Perhaps he only spoke his mind and not his heart. He wasn't looking for anything in return. He didn't mean to disturb the status quo. He didn't want to state any expectations. But then, I could read between the lines in the way he said things. What was left unsaid was up to me to interpret. Or perhaps, it wasn't. But then I thought about it nonetheless—*had-it-been-not-like-this* and *if-we-could-roll-back-time*, all that. After all, I too was human, with a mind of my own, with a heart of my own.

'He likes you! You know that, right?' Manvika abruptly says shaking the protein shake in her sipper.

Barefoot and wrapped in white towels, the two of us are walking towards the steam room. There was no one around us. The cold wet floor beneath my feet feels nice. It's been about ten minutes since we've finished our workout. It's one of those rare days when Aarav has trained both of us together. The evening before, on our WhatsApp group, we had insisted he do that.

In the locker room, while undressing, Manvika and I have been talking about Aarav. I know I can't stop thinking about him since our last conversation and she's only too happy talking about us. We have now brought the conversation inside the steam room. It's the place we find most easy to talk in.

We step inside the white darkness of the humid room. It takes us a few seconds to get used to the very dim yellow bulb light and to find ourselves a place to sit. Thankfully, there is no one in the steam room at this hour.

'He likes everyone. He is a dedicated trainer,' I say trying to act ignorant about what Manvika intends to say.

'Not like-like! Come on! You know what I mean. Like love-like!' she clarifies. She is a sharp woman. Nothing escapes her!

'You have got to be kidding me!' I say to throw her off. But inside, it feels nice to hear Manvika's opinion. I know I am blushing but Manvika can't see my actual reaction. I have to be thankful for that.

86

She takes a moment to sip her whey protein. I am contemplating whether I should change the subject. But secretly I want Manvika to continue and add more to her previous statement. I play it safe and don't say anything else, but drink my protein shake instead.

'Really? You don't think so?' Manvika asks within minutes.

'Of course not!' I pretend.

Manvika is smart enough to make this out. She senses the opportunity and drops the ball in my court. 'Guess you are right. Let's leave it.' She says and concentrates on her drink. But I know she's thinking too. I can make that out from the way she is noisily sipping away.

And suddenly, I am sure I don't want to change the subject. So I ask, 'But what made you say so in the first place?'

'Oh it's nothing . . .' I hate her for doing this to me.

'But still?' I insist and make it utterly evident now. How I've put my own foot in my mouth!

'Looks . . . like . . . someone . . . is . . . now . . . very . . . interested?' Manvika drawls out, savouring the moment at my cost.

Curiosity with denial appears like a good strategy to me. So I giggle and say, 'Nothing like that, but you have made me curious.'

Manvika is kind enough not to stretch it further. She knows, in a way, I have cleared her doubts. So she tells me, 'It's evident in his eyes, in his body language. Look at the way he treats you!'

'What do you mean by the way he treats me?' I ask her.

'Haven't you noticed?'

'Noticed what?'

'. . . How at times he hesitates to touch you while training?'

I think it over. 'What are you talking about? Didn't you see him supporting me when we did the bicep curls? We lifted quite a heavy load today!'

'I didn't mean that he's afraid to touch you in that normal sense. I meant the slightly more intimate parts of your body.'

I try to recall.

Meanwhile, Manvika continues, 'He didn't touch you behind your legs to help you understand how to isolate and contract the hamstrings. Remember? Whereas, he touched me without any inhibition. In your case, he only asked you to feel it. He didn't touch your waist when we did the Russian twist exercise. He felt mine.'

'Well, that only proves he is closer to you than me,' I say, but in my heart I know she's probably right.

'Naina, how come you didn't notice his eyes? There was something in them—a shyness I think. He is courteous to you, extra careful and treats you like a lady. He is too shy to even touch you in a way that will make you conscious. But only if you let him . . . he will.'

I realize that Aarav's approach with his other female clients has been a lot like how he trains Manvika. And Manvika is right! I certainly don't recall Aarav touching me the way he touches others. I take a rationalistic approach and wonder if he ever stepped back when there was a need for him to touch me?

I do recall how initially I felt strange when he touched me while we were training. Had he sensed my discomfort back then? Or is it now that we've talked about things . . . ? I question myself.

And the more I think, the more I want to be touched by Aarav. In a more intimate manner! The thought sends a chill down my spine. I forcefully break it and redrape my towel around my body.

'Really?' I say, only for the sake of it.

'You might have your doubts but I know.'

'What do you mean?'

'Aarav has told me about his feelings . . .'

'What? When? I mean what are you saying?'

'He made me swear not to tell you this. But I can't hold it back,' Manvika says, completely startling me. She continues, 'Last week we went for drinks in the evening and he confessed he really likes you. I had to press him hard to open up to me.'

I don't know how to react. So, all I ask is, 'You guys go out for drinks?'

'Yes. Is that a big deal?'

'No! But he said to you that he likes . . .?'

'Yes!'

'Is that all he said?'

'No!'

'Then?'

'The poor guy also said, "But what's the point Manvika, when she is married?"'

Eleven

The next Sunday I got up quite early. It was Raahgiri Day. The millennium city of Gurgaon had come up with an innovative concept to reclaim the city roads for the people instead of their vehicles. As part of this social initiative, on Sunday mornings till noon, no vehicles were allowed on a certain stretch of road. Only pedestrians, joggers and cyclists were allowed. Several radio stations and newspapers would turn up every Sunday to cover all the activities that happened as part of Raahgiri. It was exciting to see the photographs in the newspapers the next day or to hear people chat about their experiences on the radio channels.

In order to make this weekly event more happening and to bring in more crowds several events were planned as part of Raahgiri. Children and adults were invited to ride bicycles, skate, run and walk, to be a part of community leisure activities such as street games and street dancing which would often end in flash mobs. Then there were musical events for which stages were set up at intervals along the route. One important aspect of Raahgiri used to be fitness. Keeping that in mind, several forms of open air workout classes such as yoga, Zumba, aerobics and functional training were organized on a rotational basis. The gym I was a member of was an official partner with Raahgiri and therefore, every week, many of the trainers from the respective fields of exercise would conduct free classes at this event. On the day when functional training was scheduled, Aarav was the assigned instructor.

It was a set protocol that along with the trainers at least five active members from the gym would also participate in this event. The gym took that as a social responsibility and gave away fitness goody bags to members who volunteered to get up early on a Sunday morning and participate in this open-air workout.

When Aarav's turn came, I opted to participate.

As decided on the evening before, I was supposed to pick him up at 5.30 in the morning. When he first asked me to do so, I thought he was joking. But to my joy he was serious. Let's take one car instead of two, he had suggested.

'You'll also get more driving practice,' he had said winking at me. I blushed thinking about the time I'd banged my car into his.

'That's not fair,' I had said.

He had laughed.

For a married woman like me and especially because of the family I come from, it was way too early in the day to pick up a guy in my car. My equation with Aarav within the confines of the gym was one thing and beyond it was another. I had told Siddharth about my plans but I only limited it to my participation in Raahgiri. The rest of it, that I was supposed to drive down to Aarav's place and pick him in my car, I never disclosed. I would have done that had Manvika been with me. But she was too lazy to get up early.

And certainly not on a Sunday morning!

'I am leaving from my place,' I texted Aarav as soon as I started the car.

It was 5.15 a.m. and I was already in my car wearing my sports shoes along with my gym capris and tank top. The previous night Aarav had shared the Google map location of his place with me. I synced it to my phone. There was no visible traffic in the real time map. It also forecasted that I would reach his place in thirteen minutes.

Perfect!

The early morning breeze and the red–grey early morning sky was a treat. And to add to the experience were the Sufi songs on the FM radio I had tuned to. And beyond all this was the pleasure to see Aarav and look forward to his company.

'I am standing outside my society,' Aarav's message arrived when I was minutes away from his block.

And there he stood, in his trainer jersey, outside the entrance gate. Seeing him from a distance I began to smile. I am sure he would not have noticed. There was still some distance between us.

As soon as I stopped my car in front of him, Aarav greeted me, 'Good morning!' as he opened the door on the other side.

I smelled musk. *Is this his aftershave?*

'Hi! Morning!' I responded.

As he buckled up I started the car again. 'You live in this one?' I asked pointing at the tall building on our left.

Aarav looked in the direction I was staring at and said, 'Yeah, sixth floor.'

'Is that yours? That one with the plants in the balcony?'

'No. Mine is on the other side. These are the road-facing ones.'

'Ohhh!' I don't know why I felt a bit disappointed at not being able to see his flat. Yet I kept looking at the building.

'What happened?' Aarav asked.

'Nothing.' I put the car in first gear and took a U-turn.

'*Acha* listen, I may not come back along with you,' he informed me.

'Why?' I asked disappointedly. *Did he have to tell me now?*

'There's this train-the-trainer session in the Saket branch of our gym. I may have to be there by noon. But I will confirm that with you before this morning schedule is over.'

'Okay,' I said and focused back on the road ahead of me. Neither of us spoke for a minute or two. It was I who resumed the talk again. And for some strange reason I brought up the subject of Aarav's house.

'I wanted to see your apartment,' I said. We were now driving on the main road. I didn't even realize that it might have sounded inappropriate; I clearly didn't mean it to be that way. Thankfully, neither did Aarav take it any other way.

I guess it was the joy of Aarav's company that made me open up to him without being scared. And with a newly discovered proximity to him at a different time of the day, in the comfort of my car, I wanted to enjoy the conversation.

'Ha ha! But why?' he asked laughing.

With my eyes carefully fixed on the road ahead of me, I said, 'To get to know you from the kind of house you live in.'

'But you already know me well.'

'Of course I do! But then I have known you from all that you have told me. I'd like to see the other part of you as well,' I said wondering if he knew where I was coming from.

'Hmm . . . I see! But how will my house be of help here?'

'Your house is *your* private space. If I have to know you fully I have to visit your house. In the space where you are what you are. It's like in no other space. The walls of your house would have witnessed so much of you. And I would like to know that. How you keep your house, whether or not you keep your clothes properly, keep your plate back in the kitchen after a meal or not—that would give me an honest picture of your lifestyle. Like, what does your house smell like . . . you know what I mean?' I asked him excitedly.

'God! Naina that wall *waala* is scary. I have walls in my bathroom as well.'

'Shut up!'

He laughed. I grinned.

'. . . I meant it in a different way. The walls of your house would have witnessed your various moods. They would have heard you responding to your phone calls and watched you watching the TV. There is so much to it.'

'That's deep. What are you? An author?'

I giggled again at that and said, 'No! A reader. Call it the impact of reading so many books. I didn't have much to do before I joined the gym.'

'Okay, we'll see about that. Maybe one day you can come home,' he said.

I didn't pressurize him more. We drove a while in silence. It was a happy silence though.

Aarav sat relaxed. The only time he pulled himself up was to increase the volume when one of his favourite Sufi numbers was playing.

'Oh, I love this one!' he said as he turned the volume knob. He didn't even feel the need to ask me before he did that. That was the sort of comfort he shared with me, his client. And I enjoyed this close equation between us.

He hummed along , '*Kun faaya kun . . .kun faaya . . . kun faaya kun . . .*'

We related the dawn and bulb light of the Nizamuddin *dargaah* in the video of this song to the dawn the two of us were driving into.

'Yeah! Even I love this one . . .' And so I too joined him in the singing. Aarav began singing out loud. I followed suit. We both knew the lyrics well, and soon the two of us were singing our hearts out together. We were smiling at each other and commending each other's singing at the same time. Soon the enthusiasm rose so high that Aarav could not stop himself from tapping his hands on the dashboard in front of him in sync with the tabla beats. And he did it brilliantly. It took the whole thing to a new level. And when the song ended he threw his hands in the air like a maestro!

'Wah! Wah!' I cheered for him and for both of us.

'*Samaa baandh diya hamne to*. We really recreated the atmosphere. Didn't we?' he said excitedly.

'Yes we did!' I replied.

We reached the HUDA metro station. This was where I had to park my car. Beyond it was the 'no driving' zone. After parking we were supposed to walk for about a kilometre in order to reach the designated spot. But just outside the metro station Aarav thought of something and said, 'Why walk when we can jog?'

I grinned and immediately started jogging. In no time Aarav adjusted his pace with mine and the two of us jogged to reach our destination.

The freshly cleaned road ahead of us was covered with gym mats in various colours that looked like decorations. Along each of them was a bosu ball and hollow ViPR. It was a different feeling to find a road transformed into a workout arena. This feeling that you can lie down over the mat on an open road that people otherwise drive on was differently delightful.

'That's your battlefield!' I said to Aarav looking at the arrangement.

'Looks like it is!' he agreed.

There weren't many people around when we reached. But with each passing minute the headcount began to increase. It was already 6 a.m. Aarav's session was supposed to begin by 6.30 a.m. The gym's admin team helped him fix the wireless mic behind his head. He also went through the sequence of the soundtracks he wanted the team to play during the workout. All the while I watched and admired him.

We began the functional training sharp at the designated time. Along with other members from the gym, I stood in the first row watching Aarav on stage and the rest of the crowd behind me. I was worried if we would have a decent number of people to participate in the session. The peppy soundtrack and Aarav's encouraging words made everybody feel like a warrior and the group workout caught everyone's attention. In about five minutes every mat was taken up. I had lost his attention. I was only glad that his focus was now on training the crowd that I too was a part of.

Aarav first taught the people the right posture and the right way to exercise. He demonstrated the same and monitored people in the first round. Once, the majority of them had got it, he went for the circuit training. With two two-minute water breaks the overall forty-five-minute workout session went extremely well. Those who got too tired to continue further made way for others to join in.

There were happy faces when Aarav called it a day. They all stepped forward to congratulate him on a session well done. Many of them had queries and the sales team from the gym was there at the site to answer them. They had to entertain their leads. On receiving Aarav's undivided attention again, I took the opportunity to spend the rest of the time roaming on the road. We looked at everything else that was happening as a part of Raahgiri. We stopped by a music event for a while, where a college rock band was playing. We then tried out our skills on the skateboard. Aarav was good at mingling with the school kids and asking them for their skateboards. I tried my best to resist getting on one, but then Aarav wasn't willing to listen to any excuses. And so I did get on one, but on the condition that he held my hand lest I fell flat down on my face. I took a leap of faith on Aarav's insistence and pushed the roller. My companion cheated on me. He left my hand! I panicked and was too scared to put the rear foot on the ground to brake. Instead, in my nervousness I squatted on the board trying to prevent myself from falling down. Seeing my panic Aarav sprinted and caught my hand which was swinging in the air.

'I got you!' he said as soon as he held me and the skateboard came to a sudden rest. It was a big relief but I couldn't have forgiven him for leaving me in the first place. I stepped down from the board and playfully slapped Aarav on his head. The kids watched us and laughed at Aarav, who adjusted his hair and smiled back at the kids.

The Raahgiri Day that Sunday morning was like a street fair. It was all so lively, so wonderful! It was 9.45 by the time we decided to leave. I wanted Aarav's company for even longer. But sadly, his Saket plan was on. And right at that moment I had begun to look forward to seeing him the next day.

He had planned to take the metro and therefore we said our goodbyes at the entrance of the metro station. I didn't know why but I felt like giving him a hug. It was a different experience being with him early in the morning, roaming the roads and having so much fun. Something Sid and I had never done. But then I stopped short of embarrassing myself. He swiped his metro card at the turnstile while I walked away to get my car. In the vast parking lot, it took me a while to find the exact place where I had parked my vehicle.

Bad luck welcomed me the moment I arrived near my car.

'Shit!' The front tyre on the driver's side was flat.

'Oh no! Shit! Shit! Shit!' I yelled at my fate. *All the joy of the morning so far had to come to this?*

I looked around for an attendant for help. But there was nobody. Probably because it was a Sunday morning. Besides, I wondered had there been somebody would he have been kind enough to fix my tyre? The chances were grim. The first person whose face came to my mind was Aarav. But I knew that he was already on his way. I couldn't have left the car behind in the parking lot because I needed it in the afternoon.

I pulled out my phone from the side pocket of my capris. There was only 5 per cent battery left. Just my luck! I usually recharged my phone while I did my morning chores. But that day, I was out of home early so I hadn't had the opportunity to.

'Damn! You too screw me now!' I said to my phone as I quickly dialled Siddharth.

'Listen, I am at the HUDA metro station's parking lot and the car's got a flat tyre. And my cellphone's battery is dying.'

. . . 'No, I can't leave the car back. I need it in the afternoon. Please come, *na*!'

. . . 'But you can go to your golf thing an hour late, *baba*?'

. . . 'Siddharth . . . please understand, I didn't knowingly puncture my car tyre. It just happened. Bad things happen sometimes! Just like now my phone is dying as I talk to you.'

. . . 'Yes, I was careless that I forgot to charge it. But the flat tyre isn't my carelessness.'

. . . '*Thik hai* . . . then send the driver.'

. . . 'In an hour? What will I do till then?'

. . . 'Don't worry, Siddharth. You make your driver drive you and your colleagues from the golf course to the hotel. I will leave the car here,' I said and disconnected the phone, which now barely had any battery left. My anger overtook my helplessness. Bigger pains take over the smaller ones—that's one good thing about pain.

As I sweated under the sun that was quickly getting hotter, I made up my mind to go the exit of the parking lot and find out where the nearest service station was. If I could get help, that was fine, else I planned to take an auto to go home. Siddharth's driver would anyhow get the needful done once he arrived later in the day. But then for once I wanted to try my luck by calling Aarav and seeing if he was still at the platform.

'Yeah, Naina!' he said picking up the call.

'Where are you?' I didn't say a hello. I was quick.

'In the metro. Have reached Iffco Chowk. Why are you asking?'

'I am in a trouble. Here in the parking lot my car . . .' and then I heard the three dying beeps of my phone before it went off.

G-r-r-r-r-r-r-r-r-r-r-!!!!!

I wanted to cry. And yell. At the same time. The car was already too hot to sit inside, so I walked up to a shaded spot near me and stood wondering what to do next. The possibility of my taking an auto and leaving for home was higher. I was really pissed off. *How could Siddharth not have come to help me? Why was he never there when I needed him?*

My eyes filled up with tears and I felt sorry for myself for being alone.

As I looked into the distance, my eyes fell on an array of billboards marking the eating joints on the ground floor of the metro station. I was thirsty and walked to a shop. I bought water and drank half the bottle in one go. I felt relieved. The air conditioning at the food court helped me cool down; both physically and emotionally. I went to the washroom, used the loo and splashed my face with water. Just when I stepped out of the metro station, I heard somebody calling my name. Then I heard footsteps fast approaching me. I turned back and there he was . . .

'What happened, Naina? . . . huh! . . . huh!' Aarav asked badly gasping for air. Slightly bent forward he supported his hands on his thighs. 'This posture helps your body to take in a lot of air when you are short of breath,' he had once explained to me after a high-intensity training.

Without answering him, I asked, 'How come you are here? You were . . . two stations away . . . right?'

'Yes!' he said with difficulty.

'So you came back?' I asked.

'You said you are in some trouble. And then . . . and then your phone got switched off. I tried calling you many times . . . I got worried.'

Oh God! He had come all the way back for me! Deep inside my heart it was extremely satisfying to know that he had made the effort.

'And you got down and took a metro back?'

He nodded.

He had come back for me!

I could not hold myself back and did what I could not do about half an hour back. I wrapped my arms around his neck and thanked him for being there for me. He didn't make me feel awkward at all when I did that. He then took the water bottle from me and had a few sips as we walked towards my car.

'It's a puncture,' he announced pointing at the head of the nail that was embedded in the rubber tyre.

'I guessed that. What do we do now?'

'Is this the first puncture of your life?' he asked squatting on the ground with his hand on the tyre and looking up at me. I was not sure if he was making fun of me.

I recalled and answered, 'Second.'

'What did you do the first time?'

'The driver replaced the tyre with the stepney.'

'That's exactly what we need to do now.'

'But we can't do that this time . . .' I announced.

'But why?'

'Because there's no point in replacing one punctured tyre with another.'

'What?' Aarav got up from the ground in shock. 'You didn't fix that flat tyre?'

I made a helpless face, 'I am sorry!'

Aarav slapped his hand over his forehead, 'Damn!'

About half an hour later we sat in what looked like an old wrecked car-repairing workshop. The nearest gas station with a puncture repair workshop was far off and the security guard at the metro station had recommended this workshop. It was hardly a five-minute walk behind the station, in a dilapidated, abandoned area.

Earlier, Aarav had called up somebody in the gym and had cancelled his training programme. I felt bad about it; but not too bad either, given that he was going to rescue me from my current situation. He preferred to carry both the punctured tyres so that in future I could avoid such situations. I volunteered to lift one. 'It's easier to pick two than one. Forgot the body balance session?' He raised both his arms holding the tyres, showing me that he was comfortable. He implemented in the world beyond the gym all that he taught within the gym.

When we walked in, the place looked deserted. It was full of old and dead, some even burnt, vehicles parked all around. It looked more like a junkyard than a workshop. It was quite evident that it was more of a garage with bare minimum services. There were a handful of people, perhaps auto and cab drivers and the workshop staff, all from the slum. In their dirty, stained clothes they were smoking *beedi* or chewing tobacco. I could feel their eyes on me. All of a sudden I was conscious of my tank top and body-hugging capris.

Just at the entrance of the workshop, holding the two tyres in his strong hands, Aarav slowed down and waited for me to catch up with him. 'Don't worry! You are with me. Okay!' He said without looking back at me.

It touched my heart that he had understood my concern without me expressing it. I felt glad about Aarav's presence in my life in that moment.

Moreover, the way he interacted with the workshop owner in such a friendly manner made me relaxed. He knew how to deal with a variety of people.

'*Re bhaayaa . . . yo maddem ji ki gaaddi . . . puncture ho gai se* (Hey brother, madam's car has punctures).'

Aarav's local dialect broke the ice and awkwardness. Misjudging him to be a local person, the workshop owner immediately asked one of his boys to put a cot in the courtyard of the shop. His order was immediately followed.

'Was that Haryanvi you spoke?' I asked, super-impressed.

'Sort of,' he said and winked.

As I sat along with Aarav on that cot outside that crumbling workshop, I realized the change in my emotions.

How miserable I had felt some time ago and how relieved I was now! *How happy I had been in the morning!* I equated my happiness with Aarav's company. There was no doubt about it. He brought joy in my life; even when there was no misery.

'I wish Siddharth would have come running for me. Just the way you turned up for me,' I said suddenly.

'He must have been busy.'

'Yeah! Busy playing golf.'

He didn't say anything for a couple of seconds and then when he chose to speak all he said was, 'It's . . . okay.'

I sighed. *Was it okay? Always?*

'Even I wouldn't have turned up had I known your car had a flat tyre. I came because all I heard was that you were in trouble,' he said and kept staring at me.

'Really? You wouldn't have come,' I asked looking at him in disbelief.

He shook his head a couple of times before he started to nod. He looked adorable.

'I would have still turned up,' he said pressing my shoulder, and comforting me. I felt good.

Even as I watched the mechanics repair the puncture my thoughts raced in a different direction. In my mind, I kept going back to Siddharth and coming back to Aarav, comparing the two of them in various aspects.

'I wish he was like you,' I said almost aloud while I compared the two.

'Everything all right?' Aarav asked.

I looked at him but didn't answer. He asked again, 'Hmm? What is it?'

'There's a lot people can learn from you, Aarav,' I said.

'I agree!' He smiled. 'I am a gem of a person . . . you see!' I knew he'd understood what I was saying but chose to avoid the topic.

'You are! You care for people. You fulfil the responsibility in a relationship irrespective of the nature of it.' I was too serious not to mean it; and I meant every word of it.

'What happened, Naina? Do you want to talk about what's bothering you?'

I nodded. I wanted to unburden myself. I spoke to Aarav about my expectations that never got fulfilled. I shared with him about being wanted which seldom happened. For the next fifteen–twenty minutes, I talked non-stop, sharing my life with him. I knew that by doing that I had made myself vulnerable with him, but all that mattered to me right then was that I was feeling lighter with every word I spoke. Perhaps, I had shown him what the walls of my house would have witnessed. Strange as it may sound, in the early hours of that morning it was I who had wanted to get to know Aarav this way—through the walls of his house. Not just the happy part of his life but also the sadness embedded in it, if there was any. Turned out, it happened the other way round.

In the initial few seconds, Aarav didn't know how to react. But he gradually got a grip of the situation and he comforted me by patting me on my back. 'I had sensed this after our sessions. But I never wanted to unnecessarily poke my nose into your personal matters. I am not sure how I can help you, but if there's anything I can do for you, don't ever hesitate to let me know. But I am glad that you chose to share all this with me. That you trusted me.'

'I trust you, Aarav, I do,' I said and could not hold myself back from resting my head on his shoulder. I was extremely emotional at that moment. He took his time to rest his palm on the back of my head. With that I felt that I'd come closer to him in ways beyond the bond between a trainer and a trainee, beyond the bond of friendship. It was something special.

It is late evening. I am getting a haircut at a salon. This one is on the ground floor of the same mall where my gym is located. It's quite a high-end unisex salon.

I like coming here primarily for the stylists but for its ambience as well. The salon has these red brick walls decorated with pictures of international models sporting a range of hairstyles. Three big chandeliers with huge bunches of yellow bulbs hang from the ceiling, adding to the rustic look of this place. Across the length of the salon is an arrangement of workstations with back-to-back mirrors and a dressing table and a chair.

Even the naming of the workstations is innovative. The name comprises a sequential number followed by the direction on which the mirrors face. Based on the direction these workstations are called east or west. There's enough of a gap between every such double-sided workstation for a stylist to shift his trolley to either side, if need be.

I am at dressing table number 3-East. The place is bustling with people. In their trademark black shirt and trousers, the stylists are busy grooming their clients who are draped in silver aprons with the emblem of the salon. Peppy numbers, on high bass levels, stream through the Dolby surround system, installed at the corners of the red brick walls. The music makes the place even more lively and happening. The refreshing scent of shampoos and aftershave swims in the air. It's intoxicating to inhale the fragrances of a range of beauty products.

I bend forward to lift the cup of green tea that one of the staff members has just served me. Just then a familiar face walks in front of me from my left As I recline in my chair, I turn my head right to look at this guy. But he has simply vanished. I haven't been able to identify him, but I did notice the navy blue suit he wore along with a pink bow tie. It takes me a few seconds to realize. I imagine I didn't see him but his image in the mirror in front of me when he walked past behind me. The dressing table mirrors as usual continue to confuse me.

I try to tilt my head further right and look for him. But my hairdresser is holding my hair and that restricts my movement. I don't want to interrupt him. On second thoughts, I don't want to turn my head either and make it too obvious that I am checking out a man in full public view. But then I am intrigued as well. Who did that figure remind me of? His face, his name . . . it's almost there in my mind, almost . . . and yet it slips away. It will come to me any moment. I wonder if there's a possibility of seeing his reflection again.

And then I see him again. He comes from the right. This time a stylist escorts him. Oh boy! It's Aarav in that blue suit!

I immediately turn my head, disrupting my hairdresser's work. I intend to call out to him. But he isn't behind me.

I turn. He is gone again. I understand that this time he wasn't behind me, but in front of me. He passed me on the West side. I had seen him in the gap between my mirror and mirror 4-East on my right. Oh god! This hide-and-seek in between mirrors!

So far, I have only seen Aarav in his gym clothes and therefore it takes me some time to identify him in a suit. Besides, he is wearing a pair of designer glasses that make him look very different. I recall he had told me that he was supposed to attend a close friend's wedding today evening.

From behind the mirror in front of me, Aarav reappears on my left. He walks to the extreme end and takes 1-West table. We are diagonally opposite, separated by Workstation 2.

I look at him, wanting him to somehow look back at me. But he is too focused on his mirror to turn his head and take notice of what's going on at the other tables. I notice that he didn't even look at the gorgeous woman at the table adjacent to him. Come on, Aarav! Look at me—I talk to him in my thoughts.

I watch as a clean, white towel is placed across his chest. He is about to get a shave. I don't want to draw other people's attention by calling out to him and think of giving him a call on his phone instead. I stretch my arm to pick up my phone from the table but change my mind as a thought strikes me.

The idea of watching him, when he is unaware of my presence around him, amuses me. And I continue to look at him.

He peers into the mirror to look at his face. He then pulls his lips together and twists them left and right to take a good look at his stubble. I enjoy his self-attention; every bit of it. It is a rare occasion that I get to see Aarav like this. With his forefinger, he describes to his stylist the length and the shape of the sideburns that he wants.

Unlike moments before, I am now conscious that Aarav should not see me. Fortunately for me, his hairdresser has pulled out the headrest in the back of his chair and positioned his head at an angle away from me. I watch him as the guy behind him rubs moisturizer on his face and gives him a quick face massage. His eyes close as he enjoys getting pampered.

And then the next moment, the hairdresser splashes sharp jets of water on his face. I notice how his already closed eyes squeeze shut with every shower of water. His Adam's apple frequently moves up and down his throat. With every splash of water, Aarav's face twitches. How I enjoy this! Aww, Aarav! Look at you! You look like a baby braving water cannons!

The stylist wipes his wet face with a clean napkin. Aarav opens his eyes and takes a deep breath. His skin glows in the yellow light of the chandelier. In his hand, the hairdresser shakes the can of shaving foam. But Aarav raises his hand and talks to him in the mirror. I try to decode what he is saying.

The hairdresser keeps the can back in his trolley and gets the shaving brush and cream. Hmm . . . old school, I see! A wicked thought passes my mind as I see the brush rolling in his stubble and transforming the cream into thick lather—I want to hold that brush and do this to him. I want to sit on that dressing table in front of him and run my fingers in the dense lather on his stubble. I want to play with his face before I finally run the razor down his cheek.

My imagination breaks the moment my hairdresser shifts my hair to my left, blocking my view of Aarav. I am bothered by this placement. But the next second it only turns into a blessing in disguise when surprisingly Aarav's stylist turns his chin towards my side. On the one hand my hair shields me from Aarav's gaze and on the other I continue to see him through the gaps. This time I can look straight at him without him even noticing me. What fun!

His face has become my focal point. Never ever have I given so much attention to a man's face as I am giving to Aarav's. There's a pleasure in noticing his facial reactions—how his sensitive facial muscles contract and change. The sharp moving razor on the surface of his skin unearths a glowing jawline. My heart skips a beat as I watch a clean-shaven gentleman emerge out of it all. The stylist pulls his upper lip slightly to shave the sensitive area below his nose and his eyes close in preparation for the mild pain he is about to undergo. Would he do that had I pulled his lip? I guess I would have made him look into my eyes to distract him.

Just watching him stirs these feelings of desire within me. I wonder and fantasize. I want to be close to him. I want to touch his face. I want to run my hands down his smooth face. I want to rub the scented lotion. Through the palms of my hands I want to transform the intense longings from deep inside my heart into the burning sensation on his cheek. When the alcohol of the aftershave stings the cuts on his skin, I want to give back the sweet agony that he has given to me.

My imagination breaks when Aarav gets up from his chair. My face is still covered with my hair. I turn to follow him with my gaze as he walks up to the counter where he pays. Then he takes a final look at himself in the side mirror and walks out.

I want to type a message to him. But I resist the temptation.

Twelve

I jumped with joy when I saw my BMI report. Aarav had a satisfied smile on his face as he stood next to me watching my reaction. It's one thing to judge your physique with your eyes, it is quite another to have that verified by a machine. The machine is objective. And when this objective thing stated that my fat percentage had dropped below 13, I could not hold myself back from sharing a delighted hug with Aarav. The two of us then began to go through the rest of my report.

We stood in the same little BMI room, where I'd had a panic attack when I was in Aarav's company the first time. So much had changed in the past six months—the fat percentage in my body, my figure, my routine, and above all my equation with my trainer, Aarav. People who happened to see me after an interval of few months took notice of my toned body. They admired my efforts and complimented me for looking great.

When the door of the BMI room burst open, I was reminded to include one more name to this list of changes in the past size months —Manvika!

'What is it?' Manvika asked as soon as she stepped in.

Usually, she would have left by then. But when Aarav had told her about my scheduled BMI test, she wanted to stop by. Out of curiosity! And so, after taking a shower she came straight to the BMI room.

I looked at Aarav's content face and wanted him to give her the good news.

'Fat percentage 12.9,' he said softly and waited for Manvika's reaction.

'What? Oh my god!' Manvika shrieked.

She placed her gym bag on the table beside us and opened her arms to take me in them. We hugged. She was happy for me.

'So have you decided on what you are going to demand from this guy?' she asked, raising her eyebrows at Aarav.

Aarav chuckled. He knew it was coming. After all I had achieved a key milestone.

'Not yet. What do you think I should get?'

To motivate his clients to achieve their respective goals, our trainer had put in place a very interesting bargain. He would define the long-term goals for all his trainees—of course, after taking their consent. If they were successful in achieving these goals, Aarav would reward them. He would either buy a gift or take them out for a treat. The money for the reward consisted of one month of Aarav's share of the fees the client paid the gym. After deducting the gym's share and taxes, whatever money was credited to Aarav's account, he would spend the same amount on the trainee who had achieved the key milestone.

But then, these were really difficult goals, more so because we had to achieve them in two quarters of a year. To earn Aarav's reward was a thing of pride. It wasn't a gym policy. This was something Aarav had started on his own.

Once I had asked him the reason behind this gesture. And he had replied, 'It's my way of thanking my clients for making my training meaningful. You are the reason I get to do what I love to do.' *Such a fine mindset in a young physical fitness trainer!*

'Go shopping. Make him pay!' Manvika said in excitement.

I looked at Aarav anticipating that he would dismiss Manvika's bizarre idea. It was for Aarav and not me to decide. Interestingly, Aarav didn't mind! Not only was he game for it, but also had a suggestion that made the whole trainer-buy-you-clothes idea not so awkward. 'A sportswear maybe or anything related to fitness,' he proposed.

I was still not sure about it. I looked at Manvika and said, 'Hmm . . . not a dinner treat?'

Aarav pulled a chair and sat down, while Manvika and I contemplated over my opportunity.

'We will take that as well!' she said.

This was even more embarrassing.

I was anyhow hesitant about the idea of Aarav spending money on me, and here Manvika was adding to his expenditure.

'We?' I looked at them.

'Her treat is pending,' Aarav pitched in.

So, Manvika had also recently achieved a key milestone.

'She said she would use it when the right day comes,' Aarav added.

'And what was it? The milestone?' I asked out of sheer curiosity.

'0.7 hip-to-waist ratio,' Manvika said excitedly as she twisted and turned her body.

And I recalled she had told this to me in one of our steam room conversations. It had been over a month or so ago. I hadn't known then that a 0.7 was the most attractive hip-to-waist ratio for females. And there was no doubt that Manvika had a stunning figure.

'This guy is making us look sexier by the day!' Manvika said looking at Aarav. We all laughed at that, enjoying our union in the BMI room.

'That's my job,' Aarav stated raising his shoulders.

He was used to it. Analysing feminine figures in great detail and shaping them up. Carving their bodies. He was a master craftsman.

'Quite a seductive job, I must say!' I said.

Manvika and I then high-fived. We were teasing Aarav.

'Undoubtedly!' Aarav readily agreed with a smile. He was his usual self—never carrying any ill intent that would make us uncomfortable. Manvika and I had talked about this earlier and we thought the same way about Aarav. He was a great trainer.

'So you girls decide and let me know later. Shall we now begin the workout?' he reminded me.

'No, let's celebrate today,' Manvika insisted.

'You are done with your session but you are stopping me from mine?' I asked.

'When is your rest day, sweetheart?' she asked.

'Tomorrow.'

'Well, then make today a rest day and work out tomorrow, simple!' she suggested.

If I cancelled my session, Aarav would have about two and a half hours to spare before his next session. Manvika didn't have anything to do till evening. And as usual, I had no other plans apart from the workout. So, it was the perfect time to take a break and enjoy the day! We planned for a lunch treat.

We didn't even need to leave the mall where the gym was located as it had all the eating joints we would have wanted to go to. This would also ensure that Aarav could get back to the gym whenever he was needed.

As we stepped out of the gym, cancelling the session appeared an exciting idea. 'Feels like I am bunking class!' I said stepping on the escalator that would take us to the second floor.

'Along with the teacher!' added Manvika with a wink as she and Aarav followed me. Aarav laughed at her statement.

On the second floor of the mall, we walked straight into the store of branded sportswear which was right in front of the escalators. Aarav turned left to check out the men's section but Manvika insisted he come along with us.

'You are here for us. Not for yourself!' she said with fake anger.

'All right, madam!' he said and moved away from the men's section.

Manvika turned right and walked ahead, while I waited for Aarav. He made a face behind Manvika's back. I giggled seeing Aarav react like that. I guessed he really wanted to look for things of his own interest.

'What happened?' Manvika asked when she heard me giggle. She looked from Aarav to me.

'Nothing,' I said smiling and dismissing it.

'Wow! Look at that,' Manvika yelled the next moment. She was pointing at a mannequin that was wearing a stylish black sports capri with fluorescent green print on it along with a matching sports bra and running shoes.

'What?' I asked as Aarav and I walked towards the mannequin.

'Isn't this great?' Manvika asked without looking back at me.

'But I already have so many running shoes,' I said.

'I am talking about this capri and the sports bra,' she clarified as she touched the synthetic capri to feel its texture.

Even though we weren't in a lingerie shop, the mention of the sports bra, in Aarav's presence, made me conscious.

'Yeah. But . . . let me first check out all the other options,' I said and stepped away from the mannequin. I put my hands on the stack of tank tops. But I could hardly focus on them, for in that moment all that was running through my head was the mention of the sports bra. I realized then how conservative my upbringing had been.

'What do you think?'

I heard Manvika asking Aarav. *God, why is she involving Aarav in this?*

Suddenly, I felt the situation becoming awkward for me, given that we were in the store to shop for me. I didn't even have the courage to look behind me where Aarav and Manvika were still admiring the mannequin.

'Yeah, it's nice!' I heard Aarav say behind me.

Trying to save myself from further embarrassment I pulled out a top from the pile without thinking.

'How about this?' I asked brandishing it in the air as I turned towards them.

The idea was to distract them from discussing the sports bra for me. But I failed.

'*Naah!*' Manvika made a disappointed face after giving it one look.

I looked at Aarav for his opinion. He too pushed his lower lip out and shook his head.

I turned back again to pick up something different. Something else! Anything!

Nervousness had elbowed away the excitement that I had felt in the BMI room about going out with friends, some fifteen minutes back. I had landed into a difficult situation.

I would have been better off choosing a treat!

'Do you have more prints or colours in this?' I heard Manvika say. From the corner of my eye I noticed Manvika talking to the sales guy. He nodded and took Manvika next to the rack where I was standing. It had an assortment of tiny and sexy sports bras with criss-cross back straps and designs hanging in all their magnificence and commanding special attention. *Oh god!*

'And do you have all the sizes available in all these colours?' Manvika questioned the sales guy as she pulled them out one by one. Little did she realize that I might not share the same comfort level with Aarav, or for that matter any guy, that she had.

'Not all the sizes, madam. But I can check for the one you require,' he said. Manvika looked at me wanting to ask my size.

Don't, Manvika!

I tried to communicate to her to keep quiet. But it was all in vain.

'What?' she asked making it even more obvious in front of the sales person and Aarav.

Run away, Naina!

While it took Manvika some time to understand my discomfort, Aarav was quick to sense it. He had caught me gesturing to Manvika. Hence, he stepped forward—to take advantage of my sorry situation.

Not to let go of a single opportunity to have a good time at another's cost had become a common practice in our group.

'Now that you have lost such a humongous percentage of fat, you must upgrade your gym clothes. You will look great in them,' Aarav said coming close to both of us, knowing full well the discomfort he was causing me.

'I will,' I said and immediately looked at the other side of the shelves that I hadn't checked out till then.

'Ohhhhhh . . . I seeeeeee . . . you are shyyyyyyy . . . in front of . . . himmmmmm . . .' Manvika almost sang out. In her hands she still had a few hangers with sports bras.

'What?' I pretended that I hadn't understood her.

' . . . to try these,' she brazenly raised the hangers in her hand.

I felt mortified. Now I had to speak

'Oh come on!' I said and moved to the other shelf. My body language made my discomfort clear. I hoped they would understand. I didn't even look at the two of them.

How I wanted to roll back time and undo things!

'Naaaaa–yy–naaaaaa!' Manvika sweetly chanted my name. She enjoyed putting me in a spot.

I just could not focus on the stuff I was looking at. I didn't even know what I was looking at.

Manvika walked closer to me and reminded me, 'Last week, during our steam room conversation, you had said you wanted to work out in a sports bra and do away with the top you wear over it. You remember?'

'I said I want to replace my usual tops with loose tank tops,' I corrected Manvika.

'And the loose tank tops are going to reveal what you wear underneath.' She made her point. Then, drawing attention towards her hand, she added, 'These look sexy! Wear them.'

Meanwhile, Aarav too came and stood next to us and in his well-meaning but teasing tone offered, 'I can walk out, in case I am making you guys uncomfortable.' The smile on his face stayed even after he'd finished talking.

There are girls in the gym, some of whom Aarav trains, who wear sports bras, and unlike me, they don't feel the need to cover themselves. Here I was feeling awkward even looking at them in Aarav's presence. *What world am I living in?* I thought to myself. The complexity of the situation bothered me. But I wanted to step up.

'Of course not! I'm perfectly comfortable,' I lied even when my heart screamed No!

'Great!' Manvika said giving me the ones she was holding. 'Then I want you to try this green, blue and . . . where is it . . . yes . . . this black one.'

Submitting to pressure I looked into her eyes. She looked at me and winked, smiling.

I took a deep breath and said, 'All right.' I picked up a tank top and the matching capris along with the sports bras that Manvika handed over to me. I checked the size and found that Manvika had picked the right size for me, even though I had not explicitly mentioned it to her.

Inside the trial room, in my private space, I looked at the sports bras. Fashionable and stylish, they were indeed designed to make the wearer look sexy. I admired them, and for sure wanted them. The truth was, had it not been for Aarav's presence, I would have got them myself. I took off my T-shirt and trackpants that looked too large in front of the clothes I had picked.

I wore the combo and looked at myself in the mirror. I appeared so different. Was this really me? I knew I had lost weight and toned-up but the way these clothes revealed me, I felt it was someone else's body! I wasn't wearing the tank top yet. I didn't feel like wearing it. The sports bra nicely exposed my chiselled collarbones and my well-shaped stomach. Inches above my capris, on my flat stomach, my naval looked sexy. I jumped with joy. It was time to share this look with Manvika.

A couple of seconds later, I unlatched the door of the trial room. Manvika stood right outside. Her eyes widened in excitement the moment she saw me.

'Wow!' she said clapping her hands. I laughed. Then she looked thoughtfully at me and said, 'Buy them!'

Happily, I turned left and right to check myself from side and back in the mirror of the changing room. I definitely looked sexy! And I liked myself that way. The outfit was perfect. But I wasn't sure if I was prepared to wear it in the gym. *Not without a loose tank top.* I thought.

I looked at Manvika with excitement.

'Try the others as well,' Manvika insisted.

'Yes!' I immediately agreed and shut the door.

'Even I want to try them,' I heard her saying outside my trial room. Then I heard her bounding away. Good! I shouldn't be the only one dressed like this.

I picked up the tiniest sports bra in the lot. I had no intention of buying it. Yet I wanted to see how I looked in it. As I took off what I was wearing, I heard the door opposite my trial room open and close. *Manvika loved these sports bras so much that she would now trade them off for her lunch treat*—I thought smiling.

I was checking out myself from every possible angle, when I heard a knock on the door. 'What's taking you so long?' It was Manvika again.

She is quick, I thought.

'Just a second.'

'All right, make it fast. I will come back in a minute.'

Prepared to show myself in that skimpy sports bra to Manvika, I shouted, 'Hang on!' and unlocked the door.

Just then the door of the trial room opposite mine unlatched and opened. It was Aarav. Damn!

Shock rocketed inside me and I instantly froze. Exhibiting my entire upper half in that sexy tiny sports bra, I stood there in front of him in all my glory! I wanted to move my feet but they seemed glued to the ground. I wanted to shut the door, but my hands seemed stuck.

I felt naked.

Thirteen

'O . . . Oops!' Aarav was the first to respond. He'd thought it was his mistake. Within a second, he shut his door.

It was all very hilarious and embarrassing. He opened and then shut the door as if in a comic movie sequence, while I stood there doing nothing; not even hiding myself.

When I realized I was still standing there, probably looking like a fool, I quickly shut my door as well. I wasn't sure who between us was more embarrassed.

Outside, Manvika had just got back. 'Are you still in there?' she asked.

'Give me a minute,' I said as softly as possible so that Aarav wouldn't overhear me.

'Oh ho! What is taking you so long? Anyway, I want to try a few of them too. So let me go and get my size!' she said and left.

I now understood that I had mistaken Aarav to be Manvika. *Shit!* I cursed myself. Remembering what had just happened made me cover my face with my hands with shame.

It took me a while to feel better. I slid my hands down slowly to look shyly into the mirror in front of me. I could feel myself blush.

He saw me. Aarav saw me. Like this!

What followed in the next few moments was something I'd never experienced before. The very embarrassment that had overwhelmed me some time ago, made way for a hidden longing. It was a strange experience and I may not ever be able to explain it fully for I myself didn't understand what I was going through.

It sometimes happens that you are so moved by an unexpected incident that you react differently than you should. It leads you to an unknown emotional territory where you feel good about the fact that it happened—even though it was only by chance. I guess I was beginning to experience one such moment.

The thought tickled me. I took a good look at my body, focusing on my curves. There was a glint in my eyes. I felt an excitement as if I was a part of some adventure. And even though whatever happened had been a coincidence, there was a sinful satisfaction to it.

My mind was racing and I was highly conscious of Aarav in the changing room in front. *Did he find me attractive? Did he want to see me again? Maybe, secretly? Right now, in this instant, is he too, just like me, leaning against the door and thinking about this incident? What's going on in his mind?*

As I thought all that I also recalled how he'd reacted at that time. He got so embarrassed he'd shut his door quickly. *So is he regretting his reaction?*

I guess I knew a few answers. There was something different and special between Aarav and me. That was for sure. He wouldn't have reacted in this way had it been any other woman he had trained. He would not have shut the door had it been Manvika in my place. But there was this hesitation between the two of us that made things special in their own way. This sense that certain boundaries in our relationship were not meant to be crossed. And yet at times, with double meaning words and glances, which implied more than the context, we tested these boundaries. There was this constant debate between my mind and heart where the good girl within me, the traditional expectations of me, always won. But with time, the long-suppressed heart began to revolt. It wanted to claim its freedom. And with each passing day, it wanted to take charge of things. Things that the mind had labelled as sin, were now appearing tempting. There was a sense of joy and thrill in doing them.

As I took off the sports bra I leaned back against the door and watched myself in the mirror, deriving pleasure, admiring my body and still somewhere caught in my thoughts.

In the privacy of the trial room, as I pulled the capris down my thighs, I imagined Aarav watching me. The thought was arousing. I loved watching myself standing there in my grey boyshort panties, leaning against the door of the trial room. I was a different human being in that moment; way different from who I was outside that room, when I had walked into the store. The sensuous woman within me was overpowering the shy girl inside me.

In the mirror, I stared at my breasts. I admired how firm and shapely they were. I had this sudden urge to feel them in my hands. And so I did, massaging them in circles for a while. I bit my lower lip as I ran my right hand over my flat stomach; my forefinger slid into the tiny moist cave of my naval wanting to rediscover it with touch. I was getting sweetly aroused and found it difficult to hold myself back. The hand, when it was done playing with my bellybutton, crawled beyond it and slipped inside my panties down to the centre of pleasure. It had been ages since I'd done that. I wanted to touch myself deep inside.

As my fingers moved in further, my cellphone beeped. For a moment my fantasy was broken. I looked at the message.

'I didn't see anything.' It was Aarav.

It took me a while to move away from the world of my imagination to the reality of the moment. It didn't kill my joy. I was only happy to read that message. The SMS games had begun! This secret chat was again a different high. I took a bit of time to decide what to write back. And then I did.

'If you didn't, then why did you shut the door on my face?'

Gosh! I was indeed a different woman—unashamed, unabashed, intimidating a man in the trial room opposite mine. Why had all this turned me on so much?

'Okay, just a little. Not even half a second.'

'Your loss,' I typed quickly and then deleted it slowly. And then on an impulse, I retyped it and sent it before I could think too much about it.

'Wish me better luck next time!' came the reply.

Next time? Would there be a next time?

The accident of a few minutes before led to our bantering and flirting. I wondered what to write back. But then I also didn't want to go overboard. I could feel butterflies in my stomach. *Where was this going?* It was as if Aarav and I had found a different language. A language of our own—free and seductive.

I heard the unlatching of the door opposite my trial room. Aarav walked out of it. I was brave enough to flirt with him over the phone but I found it difficult to step out and face him in person.

I wanted some time. I changed into my clothes. Manvika knocked on my door again. She wanted my opinion on the outfits she'd chosen for herself. Her presence helped me step out of the trial room. I looked around for Aarav. But he wasn't there.

'Where is he?' I asked Manvika.

'At the counter,' she answered and got busy in showing me what she had chosen.

We settled for different prints, of the same combination, for ourselves and walked across to the counter. All this while my mind was occupied with the thought of facing Aarav.

From a distance, I saw him at the counter talking to the cashier. My heart felt heavy as I walked towards him. Aarav looked at us.

Immediately, I picked up a random conversation with Manvika, relaxed my posture and pretended I hadn't noticed him yet.

We placed the stuff we wanted to buy on the counter. Aarav too seemed reluctant to talk to me.

Aarav began to talk with Manvika. 'For you?' he asked looking at the second pair of outfit we had brought.

'One for me. One for her,' she replied.

That's when he looked at me. I couldn't help my smile even though I tried my best to restrain it. Aarav smiled too.

Manvika stared at both of us and wondered why we were behaving that way.

'What's wrong?' she asked.

'Just like that,' said Aarav.

'Nothing,' I said the moment she looked at me.

I guess she thought it was about my initial hesitation of buying a sports bra in front of Aarav. It was now placed on the counter, in front of all of us. And Aarav was supposed to pay for it.

She turned her attention to Aarav. 'Just because I too bought something doesn't mean you will cancel the treat. It's still on. Right?'

Aarav nodded and tapped Manvika's shoulder. 'As much as you can eat.'

Manvika was happy. She loved her trainer. I too loved my trainer.

Aarav swiped his card and we thanked him. He looked at me and said, 'Thank you!'

Manvika again sensed something between us and asked quickly, 'Why are you thanking her?'

He immediately looked at her and added, 'And to you as well. For achieving your goals.' He had handled the situation well!

We walked out of the store with our gifts and of course a little secret between Aarav and me.

Our little secret!

I lift my loose top revealing the previously hidden skin underneath it. There is no dire need for me to do so. Yet, I do it because I want to.

'Let's do it,' I tell Aarav. The two of us are back again in the confined space of the BMI room.

'You sure?' he double checks, recalling my reaction on seeing the measurement tape on that very desk, some six months back. But I have come a long way by now.

That I want the measurement to be precise is only an excuse to disguise my flirtatious craving. I hold the edge of the top inches below my breasts.

'Mm . . . hmm,' I nod twice with a confident smile.

Yet, inside I am trembling. It's just not my skin; I want to bare my heart to this man. As I offer him a sight of my flat stomach, a whirlpool of emotions builds up in the ocean of my heart. It's shaking me, while I fight against it to hold on to the earth beneath me. I somehow manage to conceal it; or at least that's what I think. And if it's still evident, I tell myself that it will only give the right hints without saying anything.

'What's on your mind, Naina?' Aarav asks holding the two ends of the measurement tape, which is hanging from his neck. Below his twinkling eyes, a mysterious smile has flown in and is perched on his lips.

I don't want to talk too much. In the moment, all I want is for him to proceed.

'Hip-to-waist ratio!' *I am crisp with my answer. I do fine with words. I don't stammer while speaking. It's just the eye contact I am having problems with. I fail to maintain one with him.*

'That's it?'

'That's it!'

'Competing with Manvika?'

'Learning from Manvika!'

'Fair enough! All right then . . .'

He inhales and exhales deeply after which he steps closer to me.

He looks into my eyes and runs the tape across my back. The skin of his hand rubs against my waist, which makes me again lose eye contact with him. I so relish his touch!

The next second he latches me in the grip of his measurement tape. Being confined in a circle never felt this liberating.

I wish he pulls the tape, with a jerk, towards himself. I want to fall over him. Damn! I want this so badly. His proximity has never been so hypnotizing. Weakness crawls up my cold knees.

But he is too busy to read my mind. He bends down and squats to check the reading. I shiver. He notices it. This involuntary shake brings along with it an intoxicatingly fulfilling experience.

'You okay?' *He looks up and asks.*

I notice how his gaze first stopped at the border of my top and then my face. I realize I am not holding my top too close to my body and that his eyes are at a vantage point. I pull it closer to my midriff blocking the possibility of a line of sight to the curves of my bra.

The build-up of anxiety of these recent moments has left me perspiring. Numerous tiny beads of sweat are budding upon my skin and turning it moist with every passing second.

'Yeah,' *I say. But my eyes don't lie. My breath too joins them to convey otherwise.*

He continues to look up and hold eye contact. I can see in the black of his eyes that something has changed in them. The way he looks at me now! It's not his usual way. Then, I sense his fingers on my waist and my back. I feel them more at this particular instance than before. I breathe heavily.

Neither of us takes our eyes off each other. Some sort of contagious trance has infested both of us.

I feel the beginning of so many changes within my body. My heart pumps blood a lot faster. Loud and clear, I listen to my sprinting heartbeats echoing in my eardrums. I feel they are going to consume me.

The tips of his fingers have made way for his palms. My waist soaked in my sweat is in the grip of his hands. And sandwiched in between the layers of our skin is the measuring tape.

Oh god!

Aarav makes me feel attractive even when I am sweaty, even when I am not wearing make-up, even when I am not wearing the best of my clothes. It's the raw me! The very me! The very who I am!

Touch is a sort of power a trainer in the gym has been granted. And with this very power, Aarav awakens those feelings in me that I hadn't experienced for several months. My hormones begin to play a game of their own. My body begins to manifest this very change. I am losing myself. I want to close my eyes and live this moment.

Something happens the next moment that makes him take his eyes off me; some sort of self-realization that summons his subconscious mind. I feel his palms parting my damp body.

He tries to focus on the measuring tape. A few inches separate my naval and his eyes. A drop of sweat drips down my ribs on to my naval and then slowly acquires the tiny humid space within it. I sense this happening. I sense him seeing this.

He fights his heart to overcome his intentions. He looks at the reading on the measurement tape after which he slides it down to measure the hip. I don't move. I don't realign myself. Only he does. When he is done, he gets up avoiding any sort of eye contact with me.

He tries to regain his composure and pretend as if nothing has happened. The next moment when he re-establishes eye contact, it is only for a microsecond in which he says, 'We are done!' His voice is husky. I can notice the change in his tone.

I acknowledge with a question.

'How many inches?'

'Wh . . . what?'

'Hip and waist! How many inches?'

'Oh yeah . . . aaa . . .'

But, he fails to recall.

Fourteen

Happiness had come sailing into my life. With every sunrise, I had begun looking forward to an exciting new day. In fact the anticipation would begin in the night itself, when I prepared for sleep. I would close my eyes with the happy realization that when I would open them again, it would be a new day, which would present me with a new opportunity to meet him. I don't exactly remember the last time in life when I had looked forward to a new day.

But then this happiness too wasn't absolute. Soaked in guilt, at times I would have to tell a lie, at times, I would only need to conceal the truth. Either way, it didn't feel right. Comparatively, telling a lie felt more wrong than hiding the truth. But in either case, it felt wrong. The price of overlooking my conscience was heavy and yet I was willing to pay it.

I had begun to make up excuses to meet Aarav. We talked beyond gym hours; and on rare occasions I even met him on the days he didn't train me. There were plenty of stores in the mall with the gym. I could plan enough reasons to visit the

131

mall and plan bumping into Aarav. The thrilling attention that I received in return from a young handsome guy was worth all the efforts.

I began to take precautions. The notification display of my WhatsApp was turned off. The chat history between Aarav and me was regularly deleted so that the phone carried just the suitable transaction of messages between a trainer and his client. Not that the conversations that got deleted were dirty or sexual in any manner—we were still far from it—but they were definitely flirtatious, or at least I felt so, given the context of my own feelings.

Often lying on my bed, with my eyes shut, I had begun to imagine him in more intimate ways than I had ever done in the days before. I derived pleasure from such musings. Yet, all this while, I knew this was only temporary; that sooner or later it will end. It has to end! But then I was that bird who had escaped the cage for a limited time. I wanted to sail high and fast for I knew the moment I touched the ground, I would be caged again. *Let me have my share of flight. Let me live my life a little*, I thought to myself to drown the guilt.

In my mind, it was the beginning of an affair between Aarav and me. Yet, neither of us had confessed of it to each other. Perhaps, we never felt the need to even talk about it. Perhaps, discussing it would have made us step back. So we proceeded, naturally, relying upon the intangibles than looking for tangible evidences to verify anything. None of us crossed the very evident physical lines. We never kissed, we never touched each other in a way that it would make us take responsibility for our action. It was a silent affair between our thoughts, our minds and our hearts. The words were never direct. They always implied something touching and it was left to the other person to interpret. Just like the other day when he had said—*I like your type*. On certain occasions, the smileys did the job wonderfully of conveying the unsaid.

Amid all this, I only hoped he felt for me just the way I felt for him. *Else, why would he spend so much time with me in person and on the phone?* That was the benefit of doubt I gave myself. Besides, there were days he took the flirtatious lead and I enjoyed the man doing so.

It was all going smooth. I had accepted this new life. Then, one night something happened that woke up my conscience and disturbed this happy guilty romantic equilibrium of my life.

It was late in the evening. I had been watching this movie on television—*Unfaithful*. It's the story of a married woman who indulges in adultery. Day after day, she lies to her husband; she makes excuses, only to meet the guy who she is having an affair with. I see myself in that female protagonist. And henceforth, it wasn't a just another movie for me. I was watching my contemporary life unfold on the screen with a peek into what lies ahead of me in future, as well. For the very first time, I get to look at my own act from a third perspective; I began to abhor my own character. As the movie proceeded, the suppressed guilt within me grew into a shame which engulfed me.

In one scene, the actress forgets to pick up her child from the school, for all this while she was busy getting fucked by her lover. That one scene made me feel sick about myself. Even though I was not a mother. Even though I was not in any physical relationship with Aarav. Yet, I could not ignore the intimate moments I had imagined with him. They could have become a possibility in a distant future if not near.

The realization badly shook me. Selfishly, I thanked god for not having taken it too far. But that didn't help me from feeling disgusting about myself. I guess my discomfort had a lot to do with Siddharth's physical proximity to me while I was watching the film; Sid was by my side on the bed. Even though he may not have been a good husband, he was a decent man. I had always known this. And just like the female protagonist in the movie, I was cheating on a husband who was a good human being. *What I am becoming?* I thought to myself. Inside I felt nausea.

That night, till late, I kept tossing and turning in my bed. Sleep had postponed its arrival. I didn't close my eyes looking forward to a brand new day. Sweltering in the heat of my sins, neither did I want Siddharth by my side nor did I desire Aarav in my thoughts. I wanted to run away; to anywhere; to nobody; no, to Manvika. Yes, Manvika! I wanted to speak to her, to confess to her.

At dawn, I woke up with a jolt, to a horrible dream— Aarav was dead. Siddharth had killed him. Just like it happens in that movie.

I was breathing heavily. The possibility of the fictitious movie becoming my reality had terribly scared me. I didn't have control on the events in my dream. But I could control the happenings in reality. Caught in between my dream, my reality and the aftermaths of watching that movie, I felt alone. Not sure of what to do, I again thought of Manvika. I contemplated calling her. But then I checked the time. It was 4.45 a.m. On second thoughts I thought I would send a message first and see if she responds.

'Manvika . . . I need you right now!' I quickly typed and sent.

I went to the washroom and carried the cellphone along with me. I had been sweating. I splashed a lot of cold water on my face. I looked at myself in the mirror. Beyond my skin, my flesh and my bones, into the depth of my mind and my soul I searched for the real me. *What has happened to you, Naina?* The mirror didn't speak. I didn't know how to decode silence for answers.

It took me a while, before I came out. Sid was in deep sleep. Not getting any response from Manvika, I considered calling her. I had only unlocked my phone again, when her reply arrived in my inbox. I quickly clicked it to open.

'It's not been 5 hrs that we fucked each other . . . U need me again? Sleep!' It read.

At first, it didn't make any sense at all. The next second, I understood that the message wasn't meant for me. *She had typed it in a wrong window*—I thought. *Perhaps, she meant to send this to her husband. But why would she send him a message? Oh I forgot! He was supposed to fly out of India this week.*

I sighed with relief and just then something struck my mind. I hurriedly opened Facebook and went onto Manvika's timeline where day before yesterday she had posted a picture along with her husband. In it the two of them stood outside the Delhi International Airport. *See you sweetheart! Bring me loads of gifts from Spain*—the comment underneath it read.

Just then my phone rang and the screen shuffled to the incoming call. It was Manvika. I picked it up and walked straight inside the washroom.

'What happened, Naina?' she asked. From her husky voice I could make out she was in half sleep when she wrote that response.

'Manvika that message . . .' I started.

'That was by mistake. Wasn't meant for you,' she said.

'I am sure it was meant for your husband.' I wanted her to say a yes.

But then, she responded, 'No.'

Fifteen

Someone pulled the door and stepped inside the steam room. I had guessed it right. It was Manvika.

She sat opposite me. I had this feeling that she would initiate a conversation, or at least attempt one.

I wished one of us had not been here. And if that was not possible, then at least I would have wished another person to be there along with us. I didn't want an awkward situation. But then, in a way, we were already in it. Not conversing with each other was in itself awkward.

Her message and call had left me terribly disturbed. Earlier in the day, while exercising, Manvika had waved at me from a distance. My response didn't match hers. Not even lifting my hand, I'd just smiled. And then for the rest of the session, I kept avoiding eye contact. On two occasions when I saw her approach me, I first faked a call on my cellphone and stepped out of the floor and the second time increased the speed of my treadmill. She got the hint.

'What's wrong with you?' Manvika finally asked when I didn't look at her even in the steam room. The steam in the room was not that dense and we could partially see each other.

I was in two minds. One to fake it and avoid the conversation and other to be honest and get it out of my system. Something made me go for the conversation. I guess, I was already exhausted trying to avoid confrontations.

I took time before I chose to speak. I don't know what had threatened me that I found it hard to say the truth that had simply nothing to do with me. But I guess, the fact was that I knew *it* had a lot to do with me for in my mind I had stepped on the very path that Manvika had been walking on for a while.

'How could you . . .' I began calm and composed and then paused for a moment. I didn't look at Manvika. My eyes were glued to the barely visible wet floor beneath my feet from where the steam had begun to rise.

The beginning of this confrontation had made me anxious. It has always been difficult for me to deal with people who are close to me; to point out that they are wrong.

Luckily the warm steam helped me in overcoming the chilling anxiety building up within me.

'. . . last night . . . did you . . . do what you mentioned.' I finished my sentence. My heart skipped a beat.

Manvika continued to look at me. I didn't look at her but only sensed this. I knew she had heard me well.

She took a deep breath. 'Hmm . . .' This in itself sounded like her acceptance of what I had just pointed out. Or at least I thought so.

I finally looked up at her and I could not see an iota of guilt on her face. Her unembarrassed eyes stared into mine. They bothered me. How could she be so cool?

'And this is the reason you have been avoiding me!' she said.

Her voice lacked remorse. *That's the thing with media people,* I thought. The daily debates and accusations have conditioned them to look clean while interrogating others. Hours back, I was going to concede my own guilt to her. But the way she was reacting, I didn't see her being apologetic about anything. I wondered what would have happened had I confessed to her! I had only desired the sin. She had been practising it.

I had chosen to be honest.

I took my eyes off her and I nodded without saying anything this time.

'I can imagine what you would have been thinking about me . . .' The tone of her voice was light. I thought she even smiled after that. For the first time her attitude troubled me. How could she be so insensitive? How could she have indulged in something so insane?

'It's not your fault to think the way you are thinking right now Naina . . .' I could not hold myself back from interrupting her.

'Not my fault? What are you talking about? Of course, I am not at fault to hear about you sleeping with a man who is not your husband,' I said sounding crystal clear. No beating around the bush! At that moment, I knew I was not just accusing Manvika, but also holding myself responsible for what I was up to with Aarav.

Manvika didn't say anything. Her silence made me retract and rethink the way I had just reacted. She was not my family. She was not in my service. I had no right to treat her this way, no matter how close a friend she had become. Besides, I again realized how my own actions forbade me from taking the moral high ground. Collecting my thoughts, I immediately apologized.

'I am . . . I am so sorry. I . . . I didn't mean to be rude.'

This time she only nodded, acknowledging acceptance. She knew I was hurt.

But then what else was I supposed to do? How else was I supposed to react? To digest what I had heard in itself was a big deal. After all she held a position in my mind that rarely any woman had held. She was my ideal. I looked up to her. I wanted to be like her. I was going to make my own confessions to her. And now she had brought down her perception in my mind. How could a woman of her stature and wisdom do what she had been doing? How could she betray a sacred relationship like this?

I didn't want to talk anymore and therefore I stood up. I re-arranged my towel and moved towards the door.

Just then Manvika spoke from behind me.

'Don't be sorry, Naina. It's just a clash between our perspectives and nothing else.'

I had already pushed the door a little but her words stopped me short of stepping out. I held on to the door handle wondering if I should turn around.

'Perspective?'

'Mm–hmm . . . yes,' she said.

Through the door that I held open, the steam rushed out. I was not mindful enough to release it.

'I accept what I wrote in the message. But not your perspective of looking at it.'

'That doesn't change anything.'

'It does.'

'How?'

'Perhaps in your perspective the glass is half empty. But in mine it is half full.'

'I am sorry, Manvika. I am not good at playing with words. Really, I am not. And I don't intend to carry on this conversation. Please! I am sorry!'

I stepped out and released the door I had been holding, leaving Manvika alone inside the steam amidst the web of her words.

The irony of my reaction escaped me. I had discovered Manvika's affair when I had reached out to her to talk about my growing feelings for Aarav.

Sixteen

The week that followed was the most difficult to deal with. After all, I had distanced myself from the very people with whom I enjoyed spending time and shared so much of my life.

Through my body language, I had made it evident to Aarav that I was only going to focus on my work-out. The poor guy noticed my changed behaviour but coped with it. He twice reached out to me, asking me if I was all right. I responded by saying that some family issues had left me bothered. I didn't reveal to him what they were. I pulled myself away from him. He didn't push me hard to tell him either.

Manvika and I didn't talk at all. It was a difficult situation to bump into her in the gym and yet not talk. To avoid this uncomfortable scenario, I rescheduled my session by two hours one day. It was by chance that Manvika too had arrived late on that day. The next day when I did not see her, I checked at the reception. I felt vaguely empty with her absence.

How had we arrived at this point! I wished Manvika had not done this or even if she had, I wished, I had not known her secret. Or if only I did not feel the way I did after knowing her secret.

When I tried to avoid her, I began to miss her. I missed talking to her, sharing things about my life with her and getting to know what was happening in her life. Besides, I had not relayed to her the tragic battle of my heart and conscience. I really wanted to vent that out. Much like her channel, Manvika always had breaking news for me. I missed her company. She used to take genuine interest in me. And when I realized this, I felt a sudden urge to call her. But then something held me back.

It wasn't the ego. It was not about who would initiate the talk—if at all that had to happen. Of course, I was the one who had made the choice of walking out of the conversation and her life. And I should have been the one to begin. But I wondered if that would change anything or for that matter would it change our so-called 'perspectives' to look at the 'fact', as Manvika had pointed out? The fact was, I didn't do anything.

I made up for my loss of her companionship by watching her news show in the evening. On the TV channel she was the same old Manvika, lively and argumentative. I wondered how many people would know or want to know about the real lives of those who brought stories from real lives—the breaking news on those who break them?

One evening, the subject of her news debate was misuse of IPC Section 354 by women and section 498A by vengeful wives and daughters-in-law in particular. IPC Section 354 gives a woman the power to get a man booked for outraging her modesty by assault or by criminal force. IPC Section 498A gives a woman the power to get her husband or any of his family members arrested for harassing her. While the law came into being for the benefit of women, some cunning minds had been misusing it to derive personal benefits.

'Oh! She did it!' I screamed with joy as I watched Manvika hold a debate on her programme. She had managed to get approval from her bosses to carry out the story she had discussed with me recently. To hold that debate was contentious because there was a chance of being misinterpreted as anti-women and that was a big hurdle. And I was particularly happy to see Manvika had crossed that hurdle. I knew she would.

A majority of panellists on her show were against her appeal to amend the sections. The female spokesperson from the ruling party lambasted Manvika on being a woman herself and yet trying to question the laws that were framed to empower women.

'Manvika, for the sake of TRPs don't try to dilute the law. You may not feel the need but a majority of women in this country need them. These sections are in their favour,' she argued.

'Yes, I am a woman. And therefore, I am worried about a large section of women themselves becoming the victim of this law in the long run. The undue advantages that are being enjoyed in the name of this law has become rampant. Is it not time that we amend it?'

She had not completed her argument when the spokesperson, a lady from the ministry of women and child development jumped in angrily, 'What do you mean large section of women will become the victim?'

Manvika responded, 'Madam this is what I want to bring to the attention of the legislatures of this country. That instead of strengthening the women, these sections are also damaging the reputation of women in this country. Here is the report,' Manvika said displaying the sheet of paper in one hand and pointing at it with the other.

She continued, '345 cases were registered in east Delhi alone last month, opposed to 236, two months back. About six months back there were 100 such cases registered. You see the number has grown significantly. It's a good thing, that vast numbers of victims are coming forward to report harassment. But the problem is the registration of fake cases. 35 per cent of cases registered six months back were found bogus in the initial days of their respective inquires. More numbers were found to be bogus in the later days of their investigations. The clause that merely on a woman's FIR, under these sections of Indian Penal Code, the accused can be immediately arrested without sufficient investigation and put behind bars on a non-bailable warrant is troublesome.'

In the debate that followed, I happened to see the other side of these sections—the dark side. I could now see why Manvika, in spite of being a woman herself, was keen on doing a news story on this.

The unchecked liberty of this law was being misused. This platform was becoming a medium to settle personal scores. It was evident in the examples that Manvika and the spokesperson from the principle opposition threw. A month back, a college girl who had flunked in an exam registered an FIR against her teacher who checked her paper. It turned out to be a bogus claim. In the same month, two maids in the posh localities of South Delhi and one in Lutyens's Delhi had filed an FIR against the men of the house for sexually abusing them. It turned out that they knew what was at stake for these reputed men in the society and that they could blackmail them. No respectable man or family would want to indulge in such cases, where it takes a few seconds to break someone's image. So they tend to settle things out of court. The higher the stakes, the bigger the price of settling out of court. The recent jig is in the corporate sector where numerous cases have been filed by female employees against their male bosses accusing them of sexual abuse. What's commonly observed in these cases is that in their recent appraisal cycle none of these employees have got an average appraisal hike.

Towards the end of the debate I heard Manvika speak, 'Madam, this law is being misused to settle personal scores. And here is why this is anti-woman. These laws are changing the relationship between sexes from cooperation into guarded hostility. Corporate managers are thinking twice before hiring women employees. For two equally competent individuals the preference is to choose a male employee. As if the marriage related transfer/attrition, the maternity leaves, were not enough challenges for women to go down the preference criteria, in comparison to their male counterparts in the corporate sector of this country. Due to such misuse of the law, the current perception in the minds of these bosses is that they want to avoid recruiting women employees, at least till the law changes. This is what I mean when I say these so-called pro-women IPC sections are eventually becoming anti-women.' She was as fiery as possible.

'So what do you want? Should we abolish these sections?' asked the representative of that ruling party.

'No! For that would not be fair to the genuine victims of these crimes. The opposition is demanding amendment in these sections—include repercussions against the woman found guilty of misusing this law.'

I couldn't think of another journalist who could handle both parts of the story with such clarity. I was proud of her and told Sid about her.

Later that night, I couldn't help myself.

'Hey you carried your debate so well!' I texted her.

She came online immediately.

'You think so?' She didn't make me feel odd.

I could feel that she too had been missing me.

'Indeed. I believe a lot of viewers would agree with you.'

'I am glad to know that. How have you been?'

'Listen, I'm sorry I reacted badly. I shouldn't have.'

'You always will, Naina. You are that kind of person.'

I couldn't say anything.

'You want to come home?' she asked.

'Sure,' I was excited at the possibility of meeting her.

'Good.'

She gave me her address and we fixed a time.

As I lay back that night, Sid snoring beside me, I thought about how I had not felt so light in my life.

It's never a good idea to fight with best friends.

Seventeen

The next evening I arrived at Manvika's apartment. It was her weekly off day. I hadn't been to the gym in the morning and therefore had not met her after we had texted over the phone the evening before.

Standing on the twentieth floor of the gigantic apartment building she lived in, I rang the doorbell.

I could hear some sort of music playing behind the door. It appeared to be Indian classical, based on the instruments I heard. I looked around. The landing of the flat itself was tastefully decorated with plants. A lot of money plants tied to strings adorned the entrance. There were a few clay animals placed decoratively on the floor and hung from the walls which together with the soft lighting gave a very cosy appearance to the outside of the apartment.

Soon I could hear the sound of approaching footsteps and the door was unlocked. As soon as she opened the door, the volume of the music in the background shot up. It was a ghazal, I discovered.

Manvika stood at the door with a broad smile. She would have already seen me through the peephole in the door. I smiled back. It felt nice to see her and also to be with her.

'So you came!' she said looking at me. Her twinkling eyes reflected a sense of satisfaction. She wore a casual T-shirt along with a pair of pyjamas.

'I did,' I said laughing lightly. She gave me a slight hug, which actually felt warm, given that it came after a cold void week.

'Come in,' she said and led me inside.

The house was barely illuminated. Barely! It was done up in a very aesthetic way from what I could see. The volume of the music kept increasing as I walked behind her through a corridor. I noticed that the wall on my right had a number of big and small photographs on it. Above the photos was a string of soft fairy lights that illuminated the faces in those pictures. These were the only source of the light in this passage. I had to stop and look at the pictures carefully because they spoke to me.

They were photographs of Manvika and her husband, together in some frames and alone in others. The backgrounds reflected the different places that they were shot in. In those images, the two of them looked happy together. But in the light of what I had found out the week before, I wondered if these photographs reflected the current emotions between them.

'Come, *na*.' Manvika's voice intervened my thoughts. There would be a time when I could talk to her about this.

'You have decorated your house very tastefully,' I said.

'Thank you. Hope you are not finding it so dark as to think that I am saving on the electricity bill.'

'Not at all,' I said.

'Some of my guests think that way. But I like it this way.' She chuckled.

I looked around myself. 'Of course it's different. But it's quite nice. I like it.'

We entered what was her fine-looking big drawing area. Even this place was dimly lit and yet it looked stunning. At the opposite end of the room, I could see two lit candle jars placed beside what looked like a king-size mattress on the floor. I could clearly make out that the music was being played from here and soon I spotted the music console.

The portion of the drawing room where we stood was decked with magnificent wooden furniture. It looked just like one of those nicely designed luxurious interior snapshots that appear on weekend newspaper supplements.

Everything around me was in harmony. Or at least it appeared so in the hazy light that erupted from the invisible source somewhere behind the false ceiling. The dark colour of the bar cabinet placed at a distance matched with that of the centre table surrounded by the seven-seater sofa set. The tall curtains all around in the room were in sync with what appeared to be an olive green textured wall. On the wall opposite the textured wall, in a giant picture, Buddha lay in peace, supporting his head on his right palm. A few showpieces and flower vases nicely filled in the spaces around me.

I instantly fell in love with Manvika's drawing area. And I realized that the best part about this room was its off-white coloured haze that was so soothing to my eyes. It added a master touch to the place. It only mischievously interfered with the darkness but never dominated it. It brilliantly kept the dark mystery of the room alive, leaving it up to the visitor to gradually discover the area on her own.

Manvika pointed to the other side of the room, where I had earlier spotted the mattress on the floor along with the lit candles.

'Let's sit there,' she said and walked ahead of me.

My heels made a noise on the wooden floor that I now walked on. That's when I realized Manvika was barefoot. I wondered if I should have taken off my shoes too.

As I approached the other side of the drawing area I realized that the wall in front of me was actually a huge sliding glass door. It looked into the nothingness above the Aravalis underneath the dark night sky. Manvika's place continued to charm me.

'This is . . . so . . . beautiful!' I exclaimed as I peeped through the glass wall. Under the dark sky beyond, I could see the faint outline of hills.

'You are looking at the Aravalis,' Manvika said.

I saw two dim stars like two shiny dots in the sky. The moon was nowhere to be seen.

'I know! The dense green belt of trees along the Gurgaon and Faridabad highway?' I asked without looking back at her.

There was no building in front of it. No road. No humans. No civilization to look at you if you stood in this part of the building. Just the jungle and the sky above it.

'So it's like an open private area.'

'Isn't that wonderful?'

And suddenly I smelled lavender. I closed my eyes and inhaled deeply. 'Lavender?'

Manvika nodded pointing to the scented candles that she had placed just below the glass wall. Their soft light reflected on the glass. Manvika settled on the mattress with soft designer cushions around her. She picked one up and put it on her lap. 'Come, sit,' she said.

I was in awe of Manvika's place. What I could clearly see was that she'd created a space for herself that she liked to live in—without anyone's influences or thoughts. It was her, right from the time I entered the house to this room—seductive and stylish.

I couldn't imagine doing that—there were just too many dominating people in my family, including Sid, who did not think me capable of anything.

'This is where I unwind,' Manvika said.

The fragrance, the music, the dim light and the night on the other side of the glass made it the best place in the entire house.

I was in the middle of untying my sandals when the musical track changed. 'Ghulam Ali,' I said the moment I heard the beginning of the sound track.

Manvika nodded.

'You enjoy listening to ghazals?' I asked.

'I l---o---v---e ghazals,' she replied, 'especially the old ones.'

I sat facing Manvika, feeling relaxed. The mattress was one of those memory foams that take the shape of your body. I looked around and saw a few stapled pages along with a laptop and mobile phone. I took a look at the headline on the paper. It had Section 498A written on it.

'That's work,' Manvika said, even before I could ask her.

'Thrilled?' I asked knowing what this story meant to her.

'Very!' she replied.

Gradually our smiles shrunk and a moment of silence took over us. We knew what we were going to talk about next.

'What will you have?' Manvika got up abruptly. She didn't wait for me to respond and walked to the other corner of the room.

Even before I could make up my mind, I saw her holding two bottles in her raised hands. 'White wine or red?' she asked.

'Hmm . . . how about tea?' I suggested to avoid the possibility of drinking alcohol.

'Tea?' Manvika repeated, making a face. 'Did you mean Long Island Ice Tea?'

I laughed. I knew it was pointless to avoid what Manvika already had in mind.

'Which one?' She raised the bottles and looked at her hands one after the other.

'Whatever you feel is a better option. But only a small glass,' I said giving in.

She placed the white one back and pulled out two wine glasses. 'That we will see,' she said and closed the door of the bar cabinet with a push of her butt.

She carefully placed the wine and glasses on the wooden floor beside the mattress. 'Let me get something to munch along with it, you keep sitting,' she said and walked out of the room.

I began to hum the lyrics, whatever I could remember, trying to match them with Ghulam Ali's voice.

The scented candles in their beautifully carved jars caught my attention. I picked one up and smelled the fragrance. It felt wonderfully refreshing.

Manvika returned with some pita bread, nachos and two dips—hummus and salsa.

She poured the red wine in our glasses. We toasted.

'To your cover story!' I said with happiness and pride.

'To our patch up,' she said lightly.

We took the first sip.

'Why did you stop talking to me, Naina?'

Manvika's direct question made me hold that sweet fluid in my mouth. That was the thing with her—no beating around the bush. Precise and to the point! Even though at times it appeared abrupt.

She swirled her drink in the glass, smelled it and looked at me.

I took my time to swallow my wine, as well as her question.

'Because I was bothered by what you were into,' I said.

'Not was. I am in it. Still,' she said audaciously.

'Yes, you are,' I said, this time looking into my glass. The idea of looking at her face while I accepted her truth bothered me. I thought if I shared what I really felt deep inside about Manvika our relationship might break again. I was there for our patch up. But then, I had to be honest as well.

Only, this time I had come with an open mind to hear her out, to be more logical and, maybe, less emotional. After all, it wasn't about my life, but hers.

'Aren't you bothered about it today?' she asked.

I exhaled, looked at the candle jar near me, 'Well, honestly, I am.'

I shifted my gaze to her face because I did not want to be shy about the topic. 'But I guess I must learn to cope with this. It is your life at the end of the day. Perhaps, one day it will stop bothering me.'

'Do you regret knowing it?' she asked.

'I do wish I had not known about your relationship.'

'Even though you realize that your "not knowing" doesn't change the reality?' Manvika said this swirling the wine glass in my direction.

I didn't know how to react to that but I asked, 'How can you be so cool about it?'

'Cool?'

'I mean so open about it? Doesn't it bother you?'

'Bother me about what? That I am in a relationship outside my marriage? Or, that you know this fact?'

In my mind, I wanted her to answer both questions. But for the sake of the already complicated discussion, I limited it to the first one.

'That you are in an extramarital affair.' I was as direct as I could be.

'Hmm . . .' Manvika said sipping her wine. I looked into her eyes. She seemed completely at ease.

'I understand what you are trying to ask. But let me ask you, why should it bother me?'

How can you further simplify something that is already so simple? How do you question the very obvious? 'Because you are a married woman. You are already in a relationship—with your husband.'

Manvika smiled. 'All right, let me help you with my understanding on this subject. And if you disagree, then do disagree with a supporting argument. Don't just disagree without having a rationale behind it. And if you don't disagree, it is clear that you buy my point. Okay?'

I knew how she played with words in her news debates. So, I wondered if it was intelligent on my part to get into a debate with her in the first place. But I knew I couldn't back off now.

'Yes, okay,' I accepted.

'Let's go step by step then. Why do you think being with someone outside marriage while being married is a crime? Don't hurry with your answer. Take your time and think.'

'Because that place in your life is meant for only one person.'

'One person?'

'Yes. One person!'

'Then where do we fit ex-boyfriends and ex-husbands in case of break-ups and divorces? What do we do with that space? Leave it empty, after they leave?' she asked.

To counter that was a no-brainer. I immediately clarified my position.

'I meant at a given point of time.'

She took a deep breath and said, 'So you are now telling me that this space is not meant for one person for life, but one person at a time. Right?'

The way she said that made me laugh. But the gravity of the discussion made me recover soon.

'Yes, I stand corrected,' I accepted. With that I wondered if she won the first point in our debate.

To claim my control over this discussion, I immediately added, 'When this one person doesn't get a hundred percent of this space, you are denying him what he rightfully deserves.'

'That's a good point!' Manvika said looking at me. She then stretched her arm to pick the wine bottle and poured herself some more. She appeared quite confident. She thought over something and then spoke.

'And what about the other person's rights?'

'What do you mean by that?' I checked back.

'What if the other person is not getting everything that he or she deserves from this one person? What should he or she do?'

Is she referring to me?

'I am sure things can be worked out,' I said for the heck of it. Honestly, I didn't have a solid argument.

'What if it can't be worked out? What if it's not humanly possible to do so?'

'Like what?' I asked for specificity.

'Like I want him to take care of me like my mom used to do, at times economically support me as my father used to do, have fun with me like my sibling used to have, become my best friend so that I can share my secrets with him. You see, I want him to give me all that my entire clan used to give me. Besides, I want him to be my lover as well.'

Manvika momentarily paused after which she continued.

'I want him to become a part of my identity, complete my social status, comfort me, become my emotional support, understand me, love me, drive me wild in bed . . . what is he—Superman? Even Superman as a partner would not fulfil my contradictory expectations, when I want him to be familiar and yet mysterious.'

She left me agape. I had no idea what to say next. Her answer to my innocent and innocuous 'Like what?' was quite a bomb!

'And to hold these many expectations isn't wrong?' I asked a simple question in my response.

Manvika didn't take too long to respond to that. 'Or perhaps, to expect that our answer to our needs of love, sex and marriage is just one person in itself is wrong?' she countered.

I chose to keep quiet for a while. Before I could counter it, I needed to absorb all that she had said. It was quite a heavy-duty barrage of words from her side. The next time I spoke I sounded a bit confused.

'I get what you are saying, but at the same time I am trying to consolidate all these reasons . . .'

I wasn't finished yet when Manvika chose to interrupt me.

'Need! Want! Curiosity!' she said.

Just those three words and nothing to support them. 'You mean when you are not satisfied in your relationship . . .' I verified.

'Well, that only justifies the need part,' she responded.

'But, if you are not satisfied in a relationship why not break out of it?'

'Exactly! I agree with you,' she replied.

For a moment I thought if she was pointing at me with her answer.

I kept looking at her.

'Oh! Don't look at me like that. I don't belong to the "need" category.' There are two more reasons I offered,' she said.

Her statement made me think about my own relationship with my husband.

What about my satisfaction in my own marriage?

How could I talk to her like this when my own relationship was not going anywhere?

I was quiet but thoughts were raging within me. I had no answers to the questions I'd myself raised.

Eighteen

The ghazal track changed again. This time it was a romantic one from a film that I didn't know of.

'Hey! Don't get lost in your thoughts.' Manvika clicked her fingers. 'Just hear me out, darling. I know what you are saying. Not many people break their troubled relationships due to social and other pressures. Couples who become parents don't do it for the sake of their children. Then there are many who don't have the courage to even express that they aren't happy in their marriage and want to step out of it.'

I wanted to move away from this unhappy relationship argument. It was obvious. Besides, she had already said that that was not the case with her. So I asked, 'And how do you define want and curiosity?'

'When you look for more, beyond need, is what I call want. When you just want to try for the sake of having an experience is what I call curiosity,' she explained.

However, her response didn't sound like a good justification to me. In fact it seemed wrong. 'Wants and curiosities don't

158

have any end. Don't you think you need to draw the line somewhere?' I asked back.

'And marriage is that line, is it?' Manvika asked.

We were quiet. Then she spoke. 'You know what, I have always wondered—why draw a line? Why can't I look forward to fulfilling all my needs, all my wants and all my curiosities? What's the harm in doing so? After all, I have got only one life. Why not live it to the fullest?'

'Criminals in jail too would love to buy into this logic and defend themselves. No?' I took the first rational dig at Manvika.

She countered, 'Comparing apples with oranges?'

'And why do you say that?'

'Comparing illegal acts with something that doesn't even fall within the purview of legality?' Manvika defended.

'Fair enough!' I accepted. 'Okay, for a moment let's forget legality. What about morals and ethics? Don't they hold anything for you?' I asked.

'They do. But then the only problem with them is that they are subjective in nature.'

'Subjective?'

'Yes! One individual's right can be another individual's wrong. It depends on how you interpret it. Feed chicken to a dog at home. You take a life to feed another. For that one dog you are right. For those many dead chickens, you are not. It's subjective. You see!'

I again felt we were deviating from the subject. It had begun to bother me that I wasn't able to properly communicate my thoughts. And I wondered why. If I believed in something, I must be able to get it out there. I brought the marriage issue back on track and asked Manvika, 'But there are constraints in marriage,' well aware that I too was about to break these constraints a week back.

And with that observation, I felt as if I had touched a raw nerve.

'That's the problem I have—this perception of constraints in a marriage! We consider it a *laxman-rekha* which one should not cross. In a sense, it sounds like confinement! A barbed wire beyond which lies what's forbidden! And it is the very nature of the forbidden to appear sweet. It pains me to be confined in a boundary and be told that only this portion is yours and the rest of it isn't. Why does a relationship tie a couple down and not set them free? Why within a marriage do you have to compromise with your freedom that you used to cherish before getting married? Isn't it suffocating that you could do so much before marriage, but not after getting married?'

For a moment, she had left me stunned. Manvika, with her words, had not only questioned the institution of marriage, but had also made me relook at my understanding of it. Yet, I could not tell if I was willing to pronounce her right, but she had a valid argument for sure. This is how society perceives marriage. And till then, it never struck me that we could question this perception.

I wondered why I hadn't heard this from anyone else. It would make for a great debate, I thought. Manvika's view on marriage was quite different and if nothing else, I did agree that in our minds we do identify marriage as an end to a lot many freedoms. Her words made me think.

'But, in that case, don't you think you shouldn't have got married in the first place?' I asked.

'Before I answer that question, tell me this. A girl cheating on her boyfriend or a married woman cheating on her husband—which one is a bigger sin?'

I pondered and said, 'Hmm . . . the latter.'

'See, Naina. I have an issue with that. On this subject, I don't differentiate. If an extramarital affair is a sin then it should be equally sinful to cheat on a boyfriend. If one is not, then the other is not. In my mind, one isn't a bigger sin than the other. As I just said, marriage, to me, doesn't bring any new restriction to my life. That's my idea of it.'

'I am trying to understand your point, Manvika. But then, tell me why get married at all then?'

This line of thought was a whole new experience for me. My perception of Manvika had changed in the past forty minutes or so. Yet, I wasn't so sure if she was fully right. My problem was that I felt she wasn't wrong either, if only I leave apart the subject of adultery.

'Why marry at all? I want marriage as well. I denounce the restrictive aspect of it and embrace the joy it brings. I want to enjoy the essence of a married life as much as I want to retain my freedom. I want to live my life with someone, grow old with that someone and have my kids with that someone. After a day's work I want to come back home to someone and share my everyday with him. I want all of that.'

Manvika was honest. Her thoughts were natural. She didn't try too hard to make up anything. And that's the reason all that she said, no matter how contradictory her thoughts were to mine, they were strong on the ground of logic. There was a rationale behind her beliefs.

It was important to me that no matter how alien her opinions were to rest of society, she was clear on her thoughts. At one point, I began to doubt my own stand on marriage and felt as if my understanding of this relationship was unclear. Yet, something in it was bothering me—the aspect of cheating. I thought to challenge her stand on this ground.

At the same time, I also wondered if somebody else in my place would have debated better with Manvika. But then, I also realized that the need of a debate is not to win an argument, but to derive wisdom out of the other person's perspective. What's the point if someone else on my behalf is able to convince Manvika, when it leaves me unconvinced? After all, I was now unconvinced with all that I had believed in for so long.

Just then my phone rang. It was Sid. I excused myself to take my husband's call.

He was home early that evening. He wasn't alone but with an NRI couple—his business guests, who were to take a late night flight back to Europe. He wanted me to come back home and meet them. I would be good company to the wife, he said, and insisted I reach home soon.

'I am at Manvika's house,' I said. But that didn't seem to worry Sid.

'You have the driver?' he asked.

'Yes,'

'Then come home. Mom can't take care of all this,' he said a bit irritated.

'Okay in half an hour . . . *thik hai* . . .' I ended the call and looked at Manvika. Without wanting to, I said, 'I have to leave.'

'What happened?' she asked. I told her the reason.

'Well, then, leave in some time,' she suggested.

'I wish I could,' I said regretfully.

Unwilling to let me go, she asked, 'Do you really want to go right now?'

I shook my head.

'Then why did you say Yes when you wanted to say No?'

'I don't know.'

Manvika looked at me with a sympathetic smile. We were in the middle of discussing marriage and the freedom it curtails. Siddharth's call just offered a live example of it. I wanted to say 'No', but ended up saying 'Yes'.

But Manvika didn't say anything. She didn't want to prove anything by offending me. She was sensitive enough and only nodded in silence. That meant that she understood.

She stretched her arm and caressed my cheek with her fingers. It felt nice. I was glad that we had got back to what we were before, or maybe even more than that after the conversation, which I was leaving now without a clear answer.

Manvika walked me to my car.

'I really enjoyed this evening with you, Manvika,' I said holding her hands. We hugged.

'I will see you in the gym tomorrow,' Manvika said and waved.

On my way back home, I kept thinking about all that Manvika had talked about. All that, in the light of the reason for which I had to leave for home—my constraints in the institution of marriage. *Do I need to take charge of my life?* I thought. *Will I ever be able to do that?*

I certainly didn't have an answer.

Later that night, I called Manvika on her phone and shared with her all that had transpired in my heart and in my mind with respect to Aarav and Siddharth. She heard me patiently. With every fact that I revealed to her, I felt lighter. Seconds before we disconnected, I remembered her telling me, 'It's natural for humans to follow love. Don't curse yourself.'

I slept well that night.

Nineteen

Five days later was the day of our anniversary. It was the third week of December and we were facing a rather chilly winter. The year was coming to an end.

Two years ago, it was on one such cold early morning when I had first shared the bed with Siddharth. I had arrived in this house after going through a long, tiring, big-fat marriage ceremony. So much had happened in those three days before that morning.

That was one morning. And today is another. The two look so different; far away from each other, farther than the time gap that separates them.

We were supposed to wake up in Maldives today. But we didn't. Siddharth's business intervened, again. The day before yesterday, unlike me, my husband did go to the airport—to take a flight and meet his clients in London. It was unplanned. What was actually planned was called off. So that it hurt less, I was offered a better word—postponed!

Every message that arrived on my phone wishing me a happy anniversary made me uncomfortable.

The kind of pain that you can't share with people is worse than one that is apparent. Worst of all is the kind you have to defend, justifying reasons that you yourself don't buy.

'It was urgent work,' I told people.

Why am I giving these explanations?

I had to sound convincing enough for others to believe how badly Siddharth wanted to take me to Maldives. But then the client wouldn't understand. The wife has to!

Amidst explaining my situation to others, there were moments when I ended up explaining it to myself. After all, I had to deal with my anxieties as well.

Why am I so depressed? After all, Siddharth and my marriage began with him calling off our honeymoon for the sake of his work. Back then, I needed that time alone to know my husband, before I settled down in a new house that I was supposed to call home. In comparison to cancelling and rescheduling the honeymoon to a later date, bailing out of an anniversary isn't that bad.

Or is it?

No, it's not! Honeymoon happens only once. Anniversaries are for a lifetime.

But then why am I feeling this miserable about all this?

I don't know. Perhaps, it's a fresh ache. I am still in this moment and this moment is not in hindsight, as is my honeymoon. Or perhaps, this time it is actually worse than postponing the honeymoon, because back then I didn't know Siddharth as well as I do today. Today, I know his priorities and that I don't figure in them. Back then, I believed that calling off a romantic vacation was an emergency, which was not supposed to repeat in my life. In our lives!

But it did.

Our relationship continues to lose its spark. I wanted to use this trip to reinvent things for both of us. I had never needed it as bad as I needed it now. This was the time I was looking forward to get undivided attention from him. When he is away from home and not with his clients. But just with me. When he is busy building not structures but our relationship. I had been eagerly awaiting this vacation.

But then haven't I got used to living like this? Haven't I accepted this to be my life?

I debated with my inner self, at times finding ways to reject my pain. At times, wanting to get over it, but failing to hold myself from going back to the same thoughts again and again. The more I resisted, the more they persisted.

But this anniversary vacation was also supposed to be a very special one for another reason. Having reinvented myself in the gym for the past eight months, this vacation was meant to be a celebration of my success. I had discovered a sensual side to me and I wanted to express it to my husband. I wanted to leverage this opportunity to move far away from Aarav, in my mind, and get closer to my husband. Away from the homeland on the beaches of Maldives, I wanted to enjoy wearing the dresses I had specially got for myself, which I could never wear in the circle I lived in.

I wanted to celebrate the body I had built with so much hard work by wearing the dresses that would look good on me. I know they made me look hot. They made me feel sexy. They were both the testimony and the prize to the gallons of sweat I had shed in the gym. Far away from people who would deny me my right to wear them or judge me for it, I wanted to do so in the company of my husband. It wasn't too much to expect.

Even though Siddharth had noticed and admired the change in me, I wanted him to show a deeper interest in me. A getaway would have been a perfect opening to initiate a meaningful conversation with Siddharth. I wanted to speak my heart out to him; tell him how these days I had been feeling unwanted. To figure out ways of how we could add spark to our rather dull relationship. To remind him of the long-forgotten romance in our lives and see how we could bring it back. And that's why this anniversary getaway was meant to be different from any other occasion till then.

But then that's not happening now.

I was trying to contemplate the meaning of my life, if there was any, when my cellphone beeped.

'How's Maldives treating u babes? ☺' It was Manvika. She had remembered! It was with her that I had gone shopping. Most of the dresses I'd bought were chosen by her. She knew how much I wanted to please Siddharth.

I looked at my watch and realized she must be in the gym at that time. The cancellation of the travel plans had emotionally affected me so much that for the past two days I hadn't even gone to the gym. I wanted to avoid any further confrontations and explanations on this subject. I tried to get over it myself before I shared it with Manvika and especially Aarav, who had trained me keeping this day in mind. What would I tell him—that my husband cancelled it?

But then it had been a long day for me. I had become sick and tired of writing a 'thank you' back to every message that had been coming on my phone since morning and concealing my agony. I chose to be practical in responding to Manvika. 'Didn't go ☹'

She immediately called me.

It felt good talking to her. I wondered why I hadn't done that earlier. I expressed my sadness. She sympathized with me.

As I poured my heart out to her, little did I realize that Manvika was sitting right in front of Aarav, at the juice counter in the gym.

Twenty

Later that day, around 4.15 p.m., Aarav called. He had refrained from calling me ever since I had started distancing myself from him. I believed in his mind he had blamed the events in the BMI room for my cold behaviour. I picked up the phone and had barely said hello when I heard Manvika's voice. I was surprised to hear her voice when I was expecting Aarav's. There was loud music in the background. It didn't echo like it does in the gym.

I realized the two were in the car and Aarav had put me on speakerphone.

'Get ready in thirty minutes.'

Manvika's voice rose above the loud FM radio she had tuned into.

'What? But why?' I asked.

'We are going to celebrate your "not going to Maldives"!' she shouted.

I didn't know how to react. I wasn't prepared for it. Yet, as we spoke, Manvika's innovative line of celebrating-my-not-going-to-Maldives made me smile. She was fabulous. She made the pain sound interesting.

But I was not in the mood. It sounded odd. What would my in-laws think? No, this was not possible.

'Thank you, but no thank you!' I shouted back.

But how does one convince Manvika to let go of her plans? She was in no mood to hear a 'No'. She was too excited to even debate it. Moreover, she had got Aarav along to back her up.

What was supposed to be the most happening day of the year for me had already turned out to be the gloomiest day of all. My in-laws too didn't put in any effort to make the day special for me. They had wished me in the morning and their job was done. On this sad day, when my family didn't do enough to uplift my mood, there were these two people, who I had bumped into at the gym eight months back, who truly wanted to cheer me up.

Should I deny them the pleasure to make me happy when no one else was even trying? As I thought over it, I realized that out of the blue it was an opportunity for me to get over the terrible day.

'Okay,' I agreed.

'Yes!' I heard Aarav screaming. It felt nice to hear his happy voice again after so long.

Manvika shouted, 'Wear the dress you got for tonight.'

I rolled my eyes and tried to remember what exactly I had planned to wear for that evening in Maldives. Manvika remembering the dress soon had me grinning as I recalled the red satin tube dress I had bought for the night. I did not buy it to wear it in Gurgaon! It would be too awkward for me.

'Nope, not happening,' I said.

'Come on! Why not?' Manvika asked.

'Be a sport, Naina,' Aarav said. 'You worked hard for that dress for eight months!'

Even though I had changed, Aarav chose to remain the same good guy. I was glad to realize this. *Manvika must have told him about the dress.*

'I am not going to wear it in front of you!' I immediately said making fun of Aarav. I wanted to reclaim our special bond. Now, even Manvika was fully aware of my feelings for him.

'I ask you to wear it as your *guru dakshina*,' he teased.

I heard Manvika laughing aloud at that.

'Which guru? What dakshina?' I teased back.

'*Ghor kalyug!*' Aarav said in a miserable tone. And I could not help laughing.

'I am that guru. We had the goal, Size-M. Remember?' He elaborated his point and said, 'Now that you have achieved your goal, I demand my price, the guru dakshina.'

That was a masterstroke Aarav had played.

I had never worn anything like that before in my life. It was going to be awkward to dress up in it in front of people who knew me. Besides, I didn't want to raise any eyebrows due to my attire. But deep inside, I wanted to wear it. It was just that I wanted to be comfortable doing so.

'Do you even know what the temperature is outside?'

'You've got a long coat with you?' asked Manvika, the very next moment.

'Hmm . . . I do. And long boots as well,' I replied. The idea of wearing an overcoat salvaged a good amount of my concerns and encouraged me to give Manvika's suggestion serious thought.

'Well, then, go for it,' she said.

Even though an overcoat would hedge most of the risks of wearing a tiny dress, the thought of taking it off at some stage still lingered in my mind.

'And you are not going to ask me to take it off,' I checked, laughing.

'Of course, I will. Don't make your dress sound like a bikini!' Manvika confirmed my suspicion.

Next, I heard Aarav laughing. He tapped the dashboard of the car cheering Manvika for being upfront and paying no heed to my apprehensions. I felt embarrassed that she said all that in front of Aarav and immediately recalled the blunder that had happened at the sports store.

I asked Manvika to pull her car over. I wanted to be put off the speaker mode and talk directly to her without any hesitation.

Talking one on one, on a serious note, she addressed all my concerns. She did her best to make me comfortable with the idea of wearing a tube dress. 'This isn't the first time a girl is going to wear this sort of a dress. So many wear it in this city every day,' she said.

'And Aarav? Wouldn't it be odd in front of him?'

'Only if you make it awkward. Otherwise he knows enough about our bodies,' she said with a laugh.

'Siddharth's parents are at home . . .' I said.

'Listen, they didn't do anything for you, so they shouldn't be grudging you a small night-out with friends. Also, you have the overcoat to hide your dress.'

'I know, but it's so cold! I wish we'd made a plan during the day . . .'

'Don't worry about the cold outside. We are going to a place where you will only feel the heat!' Manvika added.

Before disconnecting the call, she announced that they would reach my place by 5 p.m. I looked at my watch. It was already 4.30. I hurried.

Minutes later, I stood in front of the mirror in my room adjusting the dress on me. Something in that moment made me look beyond that dress, at myself.

What am I doing? I questioned my reflection.

That simple question didn't have a simple answer. It was profound enough to rip apart the layers I was hiding under and to move me towards the life I wanted to live.

The urgency of the moment took my attention back to the task at hand, and cut short my introspection. I left my own question unanswered. However, wearing that dress, which I knew would hurt the sentiments of my family and relatives, was an act of rebellion from my side. This I knew. I was happy that Manvika had made me take a stand, for myself.

I zipped up the dress below my left arm. I wanted to leave my hair open and decided to iron them. It took some time, but the end result was worth it.

I put on the lipstick that I had earlier carefully chosen for the evening in Maldives and some light make-up. The lipstick exactly matched the colour of my dress. I wore my favourite perfume and the white pearl necklace. It came with a pair of matching pearl studs which I also wore. I stepped into my long black leather boots and looked for my overcoat in the closet that had all my woollens. I was amused to find a woollen cap that matched the charcoal grey colour of my coat. I jumped with joy.

Returning to the mirror, I wanted to try the cap first. Complementing my freshly ironed hair, it fitted perfectly with what I was wearing.

The red tube dress showed my newly acquired collarbones and beneath the frill of my dress my toned legs looked good. I looked hot. This made me happy and anxious at the same time. The mirror showed a happy me.

What was also visible was the awkwardness I felt as I prepared to step out of my comfort zone. At one point I could not hold back from talking to myself, during which my heart fought a little battle with my mind.

What's wrong with this dress, Naina? Why are you apprehensive about wearing it?

The mind fought back.

You certainly look pretty. But you look sexy as well. And that's a problem.

I turned left and right admiring my figure.

Oh! Sexy! And being sexy isn't good? Don't girls, at times, want to look that way?

They do. But you aren't among that clan of girls, Naina. Remember!

I looked into my own eyes in the mirror and contemplated.

What does my choice to wear something have to do with me belonging to a particular category? Why can't it simply be about my choice, about my freedom?

And similarly others have the freedom to brand you in a certain category based on what you choose to wear.

Come on! This isn't some cheap vulgar offensive dress!

Yet it reveals so much of your skin. You have never worn something like this before.

I took a moment there. And thought.

There's always a first time for everything.

But this first time of yours was supposed to happen with your husband.

. . . who left you for his work. Yes! Right!

And now you are going to wear it in the company of others.

My close friends. Manvika . . .

. . . and Aarav, whose eyes would now get to see your bare shoulders and thighs.

Yes! The eyes of that very Aarav who probably would have noticed every inch of my figure, underneath the layers of loose tops and sports bras.

Who would have observed my behind, on which my synthetic workout capris stuck like skin. Who had squeezed and released the trapezius muscles around my collarbones to remove their stiffness. Who had made me lie on my stomach and massaged my back and twisted my legs to release the pain. All this, without making me uncomfortable for a single moment in the past eight months!

The ringtone on my phone interrupted the war of words between my heart and my mind. Aarav and Manvika had arrived. I put on my overcoat and for one last time checked myself in the mirror.

There was nothing left to be corrected. There was nothing left to be contemplated.

My mother-in-law wasn't home, which was a big relief. My father-in-law was glued to a religious TV channel, as usual, in the confines of his room. I knocked on the door of his room and let him know that I was going out with a friend of mine. He didn't forget to ask the name.

'Manvika. She is a friend from the gym.'

I knowingly concealed Aarav's name. Of course, I would not have done so if I was talking to Siddharth. But with his parents, things were a bit different.

He looked at my overcoat and long boots and mentioned, 'It's getting very cold out there. Good that you are covered up. Do come back on time.'

I said yes and left.

Aarav and Manvika were waiting for me outside my building. I saw Aarav seated next to Manvika. She was driving. He waved at me as soon as he spotted me. Soon Manvika peeped out and waved. I waved back at both of them and speeded up my walk. I opened the door behind Aarav and got in.

'You are wearing that dress, right?' Manvika interrogated me as soon as I sat inside.

'See guys! If you make such a big deal out of it, I will be uncomfortable,' I pointed out.

Manvika immediately agreed and looking at Aarav she announced, 'You are not going to make my friend uncomfortable. Okay?'

Poor Aarav threw his hands up in the air and protested, 'What did I do?'

'Whatever!' Manvika said and dismissed him.

We decided to drive down to Noida. Manvika had her news show going live at 8.30 for which she had to report at her office latest by 8.15.

'If you had to work, why did you make this dinner plan today? We could have done this some other day,' I asked her.

'Sweetheart! That is why we are going to a restaurant next to my office. I will report at my office on time. Don't worry about it,' she replied.

'And what are we supposed to do once you leave?' I looked first at Aarav and then at Manvika.

'*Arey baba,* she will come back the moment she is done with her show,' Aarav said.

Knowing that comforted me.

The two of them enquired if I had any more observations. I smiled and nodded my head. Then I told them that I needed to be back home by 11. It was important for me to tell them that as we were now going to Noida.

Manvika acknowledged this information and increased the volume of the music and accelerated the vehicle.

I sat back and began to enjoy the music. I'd earned this evening!

Twenty-one

Manoeuvring through peak-hour traffic we reached our destination. It was a high-end restaurant in a secluded place somewhere in the industrial area of Noida. At the entrance, fire torches were stuck to the wall which made a very intriguing first impression. In the dark, chilly evening, the fire provided a visual treat. We parked our car in the vast cold and mostly dark parking lot in front of the restaurant.

Manvika waved at the escorts. It showed that she had been here often and people knew her. As we stepped inside, good music greeted us. As I walked, I realized my steps on the wooden floor were in sync with the beats. I was happy to be wearing my boots which I'd bought long back but had hardly used. We passed by a dining area to our left and a barely illuminated bar to our right. It had an array of tall chairs that were all occupied. The wonderful wooden interior of the place seemed warm and stylish. Manvika did have good taste!

Aarav and I looked for the best available table in the dining area. But Manvika had something else in mind. She didn't stop and continued to walk. The two of us had to follow her. We knew we were in good hands. So we saved ourselves the hassle.

When we reached the end of the room, Manvika pushed the glass door and led us out from the lit, temperature-controlled seating area back to the cold dark openness.

I rubbed my hands thinking it would be cold. But the moment I stepped out, I was pleasantly surprised to discover the area was illuminated with fire torches, just like at the entrance. They were installed at a safe distance on both sides of the seating tables. A few tables were already taken. The fire torches naturally lit the place and kept it warm. It was an incredible night view.

'Wow!' Aarav said looking around.

I could smell the smoke in the air.

'So how's it?' Manvika turned around and looked at us.

We grinned.

'I told you I will get you to a place where you won't feel cold enough to wear this,' she said holding the collar of my overcoat. That was a gentle reminder for me.

A staff manager arrived and took us to one of the available tables. He pulled a chair out for Manvika. I figured he knew Manvika from her previous visits to the restaurant.

But I was amused when I noticed Aarav stepping ahead of me, to the other side of the table. He pulled out a chair for me. I felt incredibly good and unexpectedly shy at the same moment.

'Thank you, but you never did this at the juice counter!'

He had an answer for that as well. 'I am your guru there.'

'And what are you now?' I chuckled.

Manvika pitched in this time and said, 'A chivalrous gentleman and you are the lady.'

Even though Manvika didn't mean *it that way*, her words added a tinge of mischief to the cold–warm air around us.

She took off her leather jacket. She wore a smart black sleeveless crop top that went awesomely well with her jeans. I had noticed how on several occasions on her news shows, she would wear casual tops and give them an elegant spin by matching them with formal blazers.

After the manager had collected Manvika's jacket, he looked at me. It was time, I realized.

The fire was at an arm's length from me. I could feel the warmth. I would look like a fool if I did not take off my coat. When I did, I avoided looking immediately at Manvika or Aarav. I didn't want to make my discomfort obvious. And yet, even without looking at them, I could sense that their eyes were on me. But thankfully, neither of them said anything till the manager had left.

Manvika was the first one to speak.

'You! Look! Stunning!' Each word was followed by a pause. Her voice was soft. She meant it.

Her eyes were on me as she raised herself from her chair and stretched to kiss my cheek. I felt good. Her warm gesture made me smile.

I turned towards Aarav to see what he had to say. My hesitation had vanished. Manvika had made me comfortable. Contradicting my earlier position, I now wholeheartedly looked forward to my trainer's compliments.

Aarav's eyes were still on me. He didn't speak though. I discovered that for some reason he wasn't able to collect his thoughts well. I raised my eyebrows pushing him to react.

He struggled and managed to say, 'Ya . . . you . . . you . . . you look beautiful.'

And that was it.

I saw him shifting his eyes on to Manvika so that she could add more. If need be.

'Really?' I asked trying to make him uncomfortable.

He looked back at me and nodded his head a few times but didn't say anything.

'This guy is so awestruck by you, he isn't able to speak!' Manvika laughed.

'Come on!' said Aarav and excused himself to walk behind me to take his chair.

I too sat down.

I had never seen Aarav at a loss for words. I wasn't sure why he'd reacted so differently. I thought he would be excited and say a lot of things. But nothing of that sort happened. At least it wasn't visible in his body language.

As soon as the three of us settled down, we got temporarily busy reading the menu card. Manvika had to leave early. She quickly ordered on everyone's behalf. Aarav's reaction from moments back was still lingering in my mind.

Manvika recited a few dishes from the menu. Aarav and I merely looked for them in our menu cards. Again we had left the difficult job of deciding the food to Manvika. So she ordered.

She had just begun telling me something, when suddenly Aarav turned towards me and interrupted Manvika.

'Naina, you have never looked this beautiful, ever!' he said and kept looking at me.

It was only an extension of what he had said a few minutes back. But what was different this time was the manner in which he said it. He didn't stammer like before. He was in complete control. He knew what he was saying. He had taken his time to say it.

Manvika derived a lot of pleasure from Aarav's unexpected words. She pulled herself back and savoured the moment. She was smiling.

I was shocked. As I soaked in his words, a realization dawned on me. He'd said it! And now I didn't know how to react. I looked at Manvika. She refused to help, but then she saw my face and said, 'Wait a second. Are you blushing?'

'Are you crazy? What makes you think so?' I replied, blushing even more.

'I am not thinking so. I am seeing so!' She looked at me naughtily.

'Hello! There's still time left for your news debate show. Let's not debate here,' I taunted, only to get her off the topic.

Luckily, the attendant arrived at our table with drinks and interrupted our discussion. I thanked god. But Manvika took her sweet time to let that smile on her lips fade.

The wine was served along with the house snacks. We were told that the snacks we had ordered would arrive in some time. The busyness around the table bought me the much-needed time to get a hold on the situation. I prepared myself for what was going to follow the second the attendant left us.

'And I must thank you for this transformation,' I said looking at Aarav with artificial confidence. I had to keep Manvika from speaking.

And I had succeeded in doing so.

Aarav smiled. 'Well, you are a great student!' he said.

'But not greater than me!' Manvika interrupted, taking fake offence.

The two of us agreed with her. On that note she raised a toast.

'To the cancellation of Naina's Maldives trip!' She giggled.

'To Naina, for achieving her goals!' said Aarav.

'To you two for turning this horrible day into a beautiful one for me!' I said.

We ate kebabs and drank red wine. As soon as Manvika finished her second glass, she left us for her show. She promised to get back in an hour or so.

'I can't imagine any industry other than the media where you can go to work drunk!' Aarav said taking a dig at Manvika.

'Oh, hello! I am not drunk. I only drank a little. That too wine!' she responded to Aarav.

'Okay! Okay! No debates here. Save them for your newsroom,' he pleaded.

Manvika's absence left a void. In the company of each other, Aarav and I only wondered what to discuss. I was thinking about the events of the last few days.

'So?' Aarav was the first between us to start talking.

'Nothing. You say,' I replied not knowing what to say. His compliment about my looks was still fresh in my thoughts.

We used to talk so much in the gym. And look at us today.

So we ended up discussing Manvika. That was the safest option. That's what happens when two people meet through a common friend. They discuss their common friend. But even that didn't go on for a long time, because we weren't unknown to each other. We had known each other for eight months now and in many special ways.

Silence followed our short-lived talk on Manvika. The place was bustling with people. Every available table was taken by then. Everyone seemed to love the fire and music.

I was still holding on to my first drink when Aarav said, 'Do you have any plans of finishing that tonight?' He was going to finish his second drink and was perhaps waiting for me to finish mine, before asking for a repeat.

'That's the maximum I am going to drink tonight,' I said looking at the leftover wine in my glass.

'Another one won't hurt. It will help the situation,' he suggested.

I knew what he meant. It was a situation that we were in. Keeping the anxieties at bay, hiding certain emotions, unable to translate thoughts into better words. That evening, I continued to do things I had been hesitant to do in my life before. *There's always a first time for everything.* I recalled the war of words with myself in front of the mirror hours back in my house.

Perhaps alcohol would help me settle down in Manvika's absence, I thought. Besides, I was so used to Aarav's motivating words which pushed me to break my limits and set new ones. That's what we did almost every day in the gym.

I gulped down the rest of the wine and couldn't help but look into Aarav's eyes. Aarav looked back into mine. Neither of us took our eyes away from each other for a brief while. Then we laughed and hi-fived.

It had been long since we did that. It felt special. We both knew we had hidden our true feelings.

We downed another glass of wine. It took away the awkwardness between us. I was relaxed and Aarav and I were talking freely again. In fact, we were talking a lot by then. At one point, I thanked Aarav for being my trainer. On a lighter note, I recalled and shared how weird I had felt standing in front of the LCD in the gym, trying to pick my trainer. It was eight months back. And in these eight months, exercise had brought meaning to my life. Every day, I looked forward to my workouts, to my diet, to my body; so much to anticipate in my otherwise mundane life.

I don't know when exactly the course of conversation changed from Aarav's coaching to Aarav's presence in my life. It was the alcohol.

The floodgates of emotions opened. It all began with my comparison of the two hours that I spent with Aarav almost every day with the rest of my day. About how hollow I would feel during the rest of the day due to lack of companionship.

I couldn't and didn't want to hold myself back. I wanted to confess to him that in the past two weeks, I had attempted to distance myself from him. And so the words tumbled out. Unchecked, uncontrolled. Then something else trickled out. A tear down my right cheek. It was just the beginning.

'Naina!' Aarav took my name softly, pulling himself up from his comfortable laid-back position. 'Hey! What happened?' He was concerned and leaned over to come closer to me. Yet, he held himself back from touching my hand. It was inappropriate, he must have thought. Even though he would have done so a thousand times in the gym. But then that was his job. Things were different here. He wasn't my coach at this moment. That was the fine thing about this gentleman. He knew when and where to draw the line. But then, this time again, I wanted him to step over that line.

Someone had to fill that emptiness. If not Aarav then who else?

'Why are you crying, Naina?'

I heard his troubled voice. Underneath my wet eyelashes everything on the table appeared blurred.

'Why isn't he like you?'

'Who?'

I didn't look up.

'Siddharth,' I said.

By then Aarav was already familiar with the issues in my married life. Ever since the Raahgiri day, there had been a few occasions when I had talked about my personal problems with Aarav as much as I had discussed them with Manvika.

Neither of us spoke anything for some time. The noise from the surrounding tables showed the high spirits of the night. People continued to enjoy.

Not bothered about how Aarav would take it, I began to talk, 'Why can't Sid care for me the way you care for me . . . for what I want . . . for what I am looking for . . . the way you make an effort for me, Aarav . . . the way you . . .'

Right at that moment, I felt his hand over mine. I stopped short of finishing my sentence. I looked up at him. Beyond my tear-soaked eyelashes that now reflected the light from the fire, his face appeared hazy.

'It's my job, Naina,' he said softly.

Aarav's words left me speechless for a couple of moments. I knew he was right to say that. But then, deep inside me, I believed and wished there was something beyond it, beyond his job that made him do all those caring things. I struggled to find the right words. But I failed. Alcohol only brings out the emotions, not the eloquence.

But I wasn't done yet. I realized if I couldn't speak my heart out on that evening, I would never be able to do that ever again. The way the events of that day had unfolded, had taken me through an extreme emotional churn. The wine had liberated me of everything. I had begun to feel lighter. But there was a lot more left to be talked about.

'Yes, but then what matters to me is that you . . . you . . . care for me. You make me feel good about myself. You push me hard, not because you want to, but because eight months back, I told you that I wanted you to. You are the one who reminds me, when I forget my own goals. You scold me, when I lose track. Aarav, you keep me focused. You make me look forward to every day with excitement. You are the reason for my happiness in my everyday life. Siddharth doesn't make me feel that way. He is ambitious but he doesn't invest in my ambitions or me. You do, Aarav. You do. You are a shareholder in my life's dreams. I wish . . . I wish . . . you could play the same role in my life as well.'

I said it. That last line. I realized the gravity of it. Yet I didn't want to go back and change anything. I was glad it was out of my system.

'Naina!' he interrupted me. He wanted to say something. But then he stopped short.

I took it as my cue. 'I love you, Aarav. You complete me,' I said. Those words came naturally to me. As if they were meant to be said in that perfect moment. That not to do so would be a sin. Hiding the truth in that emotional moment did feel like a sin. I felt absolutely no regret in doing so. I rather felt I had finally given voice to all that I had been feeling in the last few months. I let out the steam through the vent, lest I exploded.

'I completely understand you. But I hope you are aware that what you are expecting is not possible.'

Just then the waiter came to our table to check if we needed anything. I immediately slipped out my hand from underneath Aarav's and wiped my tears. The waiter was smart enough to understand the seriousness of the situation. He immediately excused himself and left.

'I am sorry if I am embarrassing you by telling you how I feel about you,' I confessed to Aarav with no regrets.

'No, you aren't. I just said I understand you. Completely!' he said in return.

I was quiet.

'Are you feeling better? Now that you have let out your feelings.'

I didn't say anything but nodded.

'Good.' He took a deep breath and then exhaled, as if trying to relax. My tears had stopped by then. I could see his face clearly. He seemed to be thinking.

Then he spoke softly. 'Now that you have let it out of your system, you will have to get over it.'

His blunt words punctured my heart.

I heard them in disbelief. Even before tears could again veil my eyes, I looked at Aarav's face and said, 'Easy for you to say that. Because you don't feel this way. You say you understand. Perhaps you don't.'

I guess he wanted to speak up but then he stepped back.

All I wanted in that moment was to hear what Aarav had to say. That's all.

A sad smile came on Aarav's face. And then his face was blurred again. Tears had re-emerged in my eyes.

'I wish it was true . . .' Aarav had only begun speaking when my mobile phone started ringing. I didn't want to talk to anybody. I wasn't prepared to talk at that moment. I slipped my hand inside the purse and put it on silent.

The next minute Aarav's phone rang.

'Manvika,' he said when he looked at his phone.

I had no clue of the time. I picked a tissue from the table and wiped my tears. I looked at my watch. It was 9.30 p.m. I realized I had to reach home before 11 in the night.

'No, she is here. I guess her phone is on silent,' Aarav said to Manvika.

Manvika said that there had been a crisis situation at her office. There was a breaking news that she had to cover. She would be late. She was apologetic about her helplessness at not being able to join us, especially since she was the one who had planned the dinner.

'No, you don't worry, Manvika. We will take a cab,' he said.

Manvika's call had completely changed the course of our discussion. It had triggered the urgency to plan things quickly to reach home on time. It was important for me. Aarav tried to calm me down.

As soon as he finished the call, he booked a cab from his phone.

'How soon will it arrive?' I hurriedly checked.

'Luckily, in five minutes.'

I took a breath of relief. We didn't order any more food but ate some more of the snacks. Aarav wanted to pay the bill but I insisted and made sure it was my treat. I reminded him of it being my anniversary and that he was lucky enough to be with me that evening. Our banter over the bill got him to relax a bit.

As soon as the cab arrived, we left.

We didn't bother to finish the conversation. It was difficult to because of the way things had turned out. Plus the alcohol had begun to wear off. I had started to regain my senses. The romantic songs on FM radio bursting out of that cab's stereo were in sharp contrast to my feelings. I didn't know when sleep took over me. I remember resting my head on his shoulder. He didn't deny me that right.

I only got up when Aarav woke me up at the entrance gate of my colony.

'It's dot eleven,' he said.

My head hurts. It's the hangover from the wine we had last night. The light from the window troubles my sleep. After failing time and again to cover my eyes with the spare pillow on my bed, I finally get up to draw the curtains.

The floor is cold. I look for my slippers but I am unable to find them. Meanwhile, I discover I am still wearing my red dress. I try to recall the events of the previous night. I feel there is something heavy inside my chest. Like an ache. I don't know why. I don't remember what has caused it. But it's there. I can sense it. It's kind of an emotional clot. I guess I will figure it out. But at present, I am unable to keep my eyes open. I badly want to go back to sleep.

A bit irritated, I draw the curtains close. My bedroom is again dark. I fall back on my bed.

What time is it? I wonder.

Thankfully, I am able to reach my phone on the side table. I stretch my arm to pick it up.

A series of WhatsApp notifications are awaiting my attention on the mobile phone's screen. They are from Aarav. A few events from the previous night flash in my mind. Now I realize they have to do with the emotional ache I am feeling.

It's 7.30 a.m. by my phone's watch. I immediately look for the time when Aarav's messages had arrived. The first one arrived at 2.00 p.m.

I unlock my phone to read it.

Naina, you must be long asleep by now.
I didn't get the chance to finish what
I had begun saying. Manvika's call had
intervened. So here I am writing to you
what was left unsaid.

I understand what you had said, Naina,
and the state in which you had said it.
You were drunk. But then you were honest.

Even though you lamented that I didn't
understand you, perhaps the lack of
understanding is from your end.

It's true that off late something has
been brewing between us. That day in the
BMI room, we had a moment. We both know
this. How did it happen? When exactly did
it begin? I don't know. I didn't initiate
it. And I know neither did you. It just
happened. Things happen!

At least you could speak your heart out
tonight. I never ever thought to even do
that. You are my client. Most importantly,
you are a married woman. What do I tell
you—that I have fallen in love with you?

Yes I am in love with you, Naina. And
I won't deny it. But how do I tell you
this? When I know that you can never be
mine?

This was a known fact since the very
beginning, when falling in love with you
wasn't even a remote possibility. But so
much has changed in the last few months.

I have deep feelings for you, Naina.
And damn, they are so strong that they
hurt me.

To train you in the gym, to sculpt you,
for someone else has been painful. I know
it may not be right on my part to feel
this way for you. But then what do I do?
It's not in my hands. And honestly, for
the time being, the pain has not been so
much for why you are with somebody else,
as it is for why you aren't with me.

I had always strived to be a professional
by all standards, but I don't know how
this time, I landed up in this situation.
There are things beyond training I look
for. I have this continuous urge within me
to see you, to talk to you, to listen to
you. All the time. Even now. Right at this
moment. I want to see your smile. It's a
joy to watch you smiling, Naina! I long
for your company. Your presence changes
things around me; for good. I keep trying
to call you or type you a message only
to hold myself back. And when you aren't
around for like an entire day but those
two hours, an emptiness envelopes me. I
have become addicted to you.

I wait for your arrival at the gym,
Naina. But then the two hours of happiness
for the' rest of the troubled hours in the
day isn't a good trade-off. Not when I know
how this thing would eventually end. We

both know. There is no point of living in a dream world. And I had to make my choices. I am going to end my training sessions. I am going to apply to some schools in Canada, for further studies in the fitness domain. If all goes well, I will move there.

Please don't get me wrong. This is needed because I can't help myself otherwise. I want happiness for you. I don't want to become your problem. And now that you have confessed your feelings, I know things will become difficult. I know the next time we are together in the BMI room I won't be able to hold myself back.

I will always cherish training you. As I end this long note to you, I recall how eight months back a lady rammed her car into mine. Back then there was no way for me to even imagine that one day, I will fall in love with her.

I love you, Naina!

Twenty-two

'I love you, Aarav! I love you so very much.' I wept over the phone as I talked to him in that dark room that morning.

His expressing that he loved me was so different from the way the world expresses love. It wasn't a proposal. It didn't have any expectations. It was a confession of true love that came along with a sacrifice . . . that he will walk out of my life!

'Please don't say that. No! Please don't go,' I begged him.

I suddenly realized that I was too loud. I feared my voice might go beyond my bedroom. So I got up and walked inside the attached bathroom. I switched on the light and saw my reflection in the mirror in front of me.

Tears had left my face wet and swollen. The kajal from my eyes had streaked down and spread everywhere on my face and blended with the rest of the make-up. All that had made me look beautiful till the night before, made me look ugly now. My hair was undone. Strands of hair stuck to my cheeks. In that mirror, my face looked devastated. In that mirror, my life looked deserted.

While I behaved like a woman madly in love with a man who didn't know how to deal with such a heart-breaking situation, Aarav sounded composed. He acted maturely and tried to handle things in a sensible way. This was also the first time the two of us were openly expressing ourselves. Nothing was holding us back.

Aarav tried his best to comfort me. In that moment, I again needed him as my trainer who was going to provide me the necessary support. Guess, he was doing exactly that— trying to calm me down. This was the first time I had cried this badly in front of him, even though we were only connecting with our voices and our thoughts. I was miserable. He was sensible. It was getting difficult for him to stop me. He was generous enough not to give up. The way he had always been.

'Listen to me, Naina! Get a hold on yourself. You can! Don't let yourself break down. Pull yourself up and face this situation. You can do it, dear! You can do it!' He tried to encourage me with his words.

I was out of control. It was as if being suppressed for so many years had burst a dam in me. And in that pathetic state, with my back against the wall, I screamed at him, 'I AM DONE LISTENING TO YOUR INSPIRATIONAL WORDS. STOP IT! It's not about training any more. It's not about my body. THIS IS ABOUT MY LIFE. MY SOUL! GOD DAMMIT—I LOVE YOU! I LOVE YOU, AARAV! Don't leave me. DON'T GO! SAY THAT YOU WON'T GO . . . say that . . . please . . .'

I slowly slid down against the wall. I was on my knees now. Leaning on the commode seat for support, I yelled and cried. What was happening to my life? I had followed everything that I had ever been told, first by my family and then by my in-laws and husband. I'd never put myself or my wishes first. And just when I had decided my life was going to be the way it was, things had begun to change. I'd found a new life, friends, an identity away from everyone. I'd found love!

And now I couldn't be with the one I loved.

My nose had blocked up from all the crying and I was gasping for breath. I was trembling with emotions that were now overflowing through my eyes.

Aarav was still on the line and from what I could make out, very worried about me. 'I love you too, Naina. I do! And you know that well. I need you so badly in my life. But sweetheart! Try to understand! Love should bring happiness in our lives and not misery. It should not make our lives complicated. And in this case we will not put my life in jeopardy. It's yours we are going to ruin. How do I do this to you?'

All that I had taken away after watching *Unfaithful* was now lying in the recycle bin of my mind. It is a human tendency to recoil to the most comfortable state! And my comfort lay in being closer to Aarav. Not distancing myself from him. What I wanted had again become my priority. What my conscience suggested took a backseat. My behaviour overrode my values. Again!

'I don't know that, Aarav. I don't want to think. I am not in a position to do that. Right now, I want to listen to my heart. I am done listening to my mind. For the first time in my life I have fallen in love. Do you understand what that means to me? How does it feel to be in love for the first time? This . . . this . . . whole sense of fulfilment that my three years of marriage could not provide me. This consciousness of being desired . . . being wanted . . . by someone? How do I let this go and why do I let this go? I deserve happiness too.'

Aarav was as much in love with me as I was with him. But for him love couldn't override the logic in his mind. 'Of course you deserve happiness, Naina,' he said, but he didn't approve of the way I wanted it. I didn't know exactly what I wanted to do with my life. Perhaps, I wanted the status quo to persist. My vision was short-term. Aarav felt there was no way I would ultimately derive happiness out of this love that would bring misery to our family and the people we cared about.

Right beside the commode seat, in my bathroom, I was caught in the most difficult situation of my life. I thought of Manvika and her logical love. I compared it with my emotional love. I tried to draw parallels between the two. It all made so much sense now. I too wanted to live a life that I cherish living, one that was satisfying.

'You will always have to hide our love from Siddharth. Therefore, you will always feel guilty in this extramarital affair. Our love will always be adultery in your conscience. It will never give you the fullness you are looking for. Try to visualize this, Naina.'

Aarav's words only brought back memories of my conversations with Manvika. I wanted to justify my stand.

'Will your husband ever approve of this if he gets to know?' he asked.

My silence only confirmed the obvious. Aarav said, 'You can't have both of us. It has to be one of us. The change that we want is so disruptive that it will break so many equations in our lives; a lot more in yours than mine. It is a big, big cost for you to pay. You are inviting a tornado that will destroy everything that comes in its way. Are you prepared to do that? Will you ever be in a position to call off your marriage?'

Aarav was trying to clear up the picture for me. But in the emotional mess that I was in, all I chose to see was the fact that he had dropped the ball in my court. And so I asked him, 'Do you want me, Aarav?'

'Why are you asking this? Of course I do.'

'Then why are you asking only me to take a stand? What about you?'

'I stand by you, Naina. In everything we do. But the question is of your choice—do you want to walk out of your marriage? It's a really difficult question. I believe the most difficult one of your life till now? And therefore, I don't want to push you to take a decision. No matter what you decide, I will stand by you.'

Indeed it was the most difficult question I'd ever faced in my life. I didn't know the answer. I didn't even want to think of letting Aarav walk out of my life. But on the other end I wasn't prepared to do the needful. *What do I tell Siddharth? I want a divorce? What do I tell my own parents? That I had fallen in love with a man who is not my husband? Even if I managed to tell them this, would they let me do what I wanted? There were several lives at stake here.*

'I don't have an answer ready. But I will plan out something. Together we can plan out something. Just . . . just . . . give me some time. Please! Don't just leave me like this. Please!'

My desperate hunger for love was making me short-sighted. I had become too insecure to walk away from the only oasis in the desert of my life. Even though its discovery was unintentional. I had long coped with my situation without it. I had learned to live without it. But having discovered it now I didn't want to be left thirsty again.

Aarav didn't push me too hard. He had his own battle to fight as well. He too was a man who desired a woman. Curbing his own desires, he was selflessly advocating what was good for me. I only wished I had met him earlier.

When I calmed down a bit we began talking about our lives henceforth. We decided to put the decision on a back burner. It was momentary though. Call me selfish in love, but I wanted to live fully in that borrowed time before reality hit me again and I had to make my choice. I knew I was going to talk about this with Manvika. I needed her.

'But nothing changes. You are not going to Canada. And we will continue the training,' I reminded Aarav.

He confirmed that the Canada plan was anyhow a few months away. So I need not be worried. However, he was of the view that we should not go ahead with the training.

'Let's take a break for a week. And we will resume after that,' he suggested.

But I was so smitten in love that I failed to see the positive side of his suggestion and said sarcastically, 'So that you can avoid me?'

For the first time ever I heard him losing his cool.

'No, god dammit! So that we can settle down! Emotionally! What do you think? This is easy for me—to avoid you? You are gravely mistaken, Naina. You don't have a sense of how bad my situation is. Don't forget I am a man and I realize that the woman I am in love with is married to another man.'

But how could I have settled down? Being away from Aarav would have only kept me longing for him. It would have only added more fuel to the fire within me. I would have craved for his presence around me, for his voice, for his touch. His argument missed the whole point. Seeing him, now that we had confessed our love for each, would bring solace. Only that would enable us to settle down emotionally, was what I thought.

Our different points of view led to a debate. Our first ever clash of opinions was on the point that we loved each other. Quite a complicated love this was!

I tried explaining my thoughts to him. But when he stubbornly stuck to what he thought best, in the heat of the moment, I ended up saying something that I shouldn't have.

'I am your client! I insist that we do the session tomorrow. There's a week left for the month to end. I will not renew the personal training membership next month.'

Love makes you do stupid things. It even makes you do insanely stupid things.

There was pin-drop silence at the other end. I could hear only the sound of my own breathing that echoed in the bathroom. I immediately regretted what I'd said. I wish I could've taken all that back. My words must have hurt him terribly.

The next moment I heard him say, 'Yes, madam!'

It is the day after Aarav and I last spoke, when he didn't want me to visit the gym for a week, at least, but I had insisted otherwise.

There are only about half a dozen people in the gym. It's lunch time. Most of the trainers and housekeeping staff are out on a break. I came in late today.

Aarav and I are in the functional area. Everybody else, among the thin crowd, is either in the cardio zone or in the weight training section. These two sections are at the opposite end of the gym to where we are.

Aarav isn't speaking properly with me. His attitude hurts me.

I am in the middle of circuit training. It's a mix of strength training and core exercises. Four in total with only a 20-second break in between. It's rigorous. Aarav has made it more difficult by increasing the resistance levels. He is punishing me for something. I don't exactly understand what.

I haven't eaten enough since the morning. I don't tell Aarav about it. I don't even complain to him that I am unable to keep up with the difficult training he is making me undergo. There is no need to tell. It's evident.

But he chooses to ignore it. 'Come on! Move fast!' Aarav screams.

I fail to wave the battle ropes and hit them on the floor as he keeps count. I am falling behind. I am losing my grip on the ropes. Yet I continue.

It's more out of my frustration than my willingness. I want to pin my anger against his!

A pool of my sweat forms on the floor. My heart beats awfully fast. I am panting. I need air. A lot of it. I inhale and exhale from my mouth. Just as I have been taught by Aarav. I drop on my knees.

'Not now. Ten more to go,' he says.

Why is he doing this to me? He knows I won't give up unless he asks me to. He knows it. And yet . . .

'Get up! Get up!' he shouts.

His insensitivity amplifies my pain. The emotional pain takes over the physical pain. I decide to finish the set. I pull myself up. I can't believe I am doing this. All I can see are the battle ropes in my hands. That's the only thing in focus and the rest is all blurred. Something echoes in my mind. Those words.

'. . . IT AIN'T HOW HARD YOU ARE HIT . . .' from Rocky '. . . IT'S HOW HARD YOU CAN GET HIT . . .' Aarav's favourite motivational words give me strength to give it back to him. '. . . AND KEEP . . . MOVING . . . FORWARD . . .' I repeat them in a loop in my mind.

'. . . AND . . . KEEP MOVING FORWARD . . .' Every time I say this to myself, I wave the battle ropes and hit them hard on the floor. Every time I do so, sweat spills off my face on to the pool on the ground.

Suddenly my ears seem blocked—the music in the gym, Aarav's instructions and the other noises around—all of it abruptly dies out. Something has happened to me. There is this churn in my stomach muscles and this desperate need for air. I am drowsy. I am barely able to stand.

'Aaaraaavvv!' I shout. And darkness engulfs me.

Some time has passed. I don't know how much.

The splash of water on my face leaves me uncomfortable. My head is rested on somebody's lap. I look up to see the face. It's Aarav.

I still can't hear properly. There are tears in his eyes. He is saying something. It's going to take me a while to make sense of things.

And then suddenly my body restores my hearing ability. Aarav is apologizing. I hear him saying sorry so many times. I recall everything. With Aarav's help, I sit up.

He offers me water to drink. I drink.

'Did I faint?' I ask. My voice is hoarse.

He is barely able to speak now. His face is still soaked in tears. He only nods. I had heard him crying on the phone the day before. This is the first time I am seeing him cry. And he doesn't look good crying.

'I am so sorry, Naina.' His words sound like a whisper.

I look into his eyes with compassion. I say to him in a soft voice, 'Will you do this again to me?'

He throws his arms around me and hugs my sweaty and water-soaked body. 'Never again,' he whispers in my ear.

It feels so good to be in his arms like this. After all that has happened . . .

He holds my face in his hands and looks into my eyes and repeats, 'Never ever again!' And he kisses my forehead.

I look into his eyes. I have absolutely no idea what I am going to do now. My mind doesn't have any control over my body. In the heat of emotions I touch my lips with his.

Twenty-three

The following week Aarav left Gurgaon, for good.

That one kiss between us was the testimony of the dangerous territory our relationship had entered into. We were only lucky that no one had noticed us kissing. If that's what we could do to each other in an open gym, the possibilities of what lay ahead for us were infinite. Aarav had decided to pull the plug before I ended up paying a heavy cost for it.

He was right at his part to do so. After all, he had the courage to face his family and take a stand on why he wanted to marry a woman who had been married earlier.

I was the one who wasn't brave enough. I had left him no option but to step back.

I didn't have the courage to change the status quo. I could not undo the equations of my relationships. I felt one can never undo relationships. We can only break them—break in a way that shatters many people's hearts for the sake of your own.

Aarav was right all along! I had not realized how difficult it would be for me to break away from my existing relationship with Sid and to discuss only about my happiness. I wanted to do it, yet I could not do it. I don't know why, but I didn't have the guts to claim the life I wanted to live. I was an educated, urban woman, but I was not an independent woman. I could not rebel against my own family who brought me up with so much love. I belonged to a well-to-do family, but I wasn't economically and socially independent. Several factors added up and discouraged me.

I should have fought that battle for the sake of my one and only life. 'You've got only one life,' Manvika would always say talking about the way she lived her life. As time passed by I realized that everyone around me lived their lives in the manner they wanted to live. My mother-in-law continued to control the house as she wanted to run it her way. My father-in-law was busy with his friends' circle. Siddharth continued to be obsessed with expanding his business. It was just I who could not voice my feelings and stand up for what I wanted.

Aarav wanted a relationship that he didn't need to hide from his near and dear ones; a relationship that was not based on cheating. He was professional enough to finish my training sessions. He did so for all his clients. In the resignation letter he submitted, he wrote that he wanted to focus on his studies in order to apply for colleges in Canada. And therefore, he wanted to go back to Gwalior, his hometown, to plan forward.

Even though it was only for a short span, Aarav and I had a love story. I don't think the time frame mattered much. But what really mattered was the emotional depth of it. Besides, for me, it was my first time. My first love! Therefore, it was immensely special. It had to be!

I loved him. And there is no worse feeling in this world than to see the one you love the most, walk away from you. I lived that moment and died tiny little deaths with every step that he took to move away from me.

Call it an irony but our final goodbye happened at the same spot where we had bumped into each other for the very first time nine months back.

I had come to the parking lot of the mall to say goodbye. Manvika had made everyone say his or her final goodbyes to Aarav at the reception of the gym. She had planned Aarav's farewell. I wasn't a part of it. Manvika wanted to give both of us a moment together, to say the final words. And so she made sure no one accompanied Aarav in the elevator to the parking lot.

The two of us stood some distance away from the exit ramp. Other than the ignition of a few engines—the only signal of life in that lot—a deathly silence pervaded the basement.

We were seeing each other, perhaps, for the last time. The possibility of meeting after that was going to be rare.

'This is it!' I fought against my heavy heart and managed to say just that. I feared I was going to cry any moment. It was only a matter of time now.

Aarav sighed—a dreadful acceptance of our circumstances and slowly nodded his head. He tried to force a smile, but failed. For a moment I thought between us he was going to cry first. He had the saddest eyes I've ever seen.

But my trainer possessed the willpower to not give up so easily. He thought it was wise to recall a humorous moment and cheer me up.

'You didn't run into anybody else's car did you?' He chuckled pointing at the ramp.

It only made the situation more pathetic for it brought back memories.

I felt I wouldn't be able to speak. So I shook my head and smiled.

'So I was the only one?'

I nodded, not able to hold back the tears any more. *You were the only one.*

Our love story wasn't one-sided. In the initial months Manvika had told me many times about Aarav's feelings. Yet, back then, I thought he didn't want me as badly as I did. But I was wrong. It was an emotionally tumultuous week, which included what I can claim to be our first kiss. Aarav had opened up to me and we had talked about everything that we had ever wanted to. He knew he had to share all that he felt for me. I believe he did that because he knew he was going to go away from me. Forever! And that he didn't want to carry anything unsaid along with him.

I learnt that our feelings for each other were mutual. So were our desires. Later in the day, after our kiss at the gym, we had met at a coffee shop on the ground floor of the mall. We were desperate to connect and it was hugely important for us to share and talk about each other's lives and feelings. Else the unsaid, the untold would have consumed both of us. Manvika came to my rescue when she heard it from me first. I could not have reached out to anybody else. On the very day I kissed him in the gym, Manvika advised both of us to talk. In the evening, I drove down to the mall for the second time that day.

When I faced him in that coffee shop, I wasn't even a bit embarrassed for my behaviour a couple of hours back.

'You don't have to feel bad about anything,' he said. Then he told me that even though he hadn't initiated that kiss, he was going to remember it for a long time. He said he had wanted to kiss me a couple of times. Like when I'd been angry with him for looking at the fashion channel and staring at the half nude models. He thought I looked cute, but he couldn't do it. He said he wanted to kiss me every time we were close doing upper body exercises and also when I looked exhausted and yet tried to finish the sets. I blushed but I also wished that we could have kissed when he had wanted to. Nobody had ever said this to me! I looked at him. Through his eyes I was looking deep into his heart, which he had begun to bare to me.

When I asked him if he would want to kiss me again, Aarav stopped for a moment. But he continued to look at me, at my lips and I knew! He said, 'I wish I could! But then I want to kiss that Naina who belongs to me.'

Someone in the coffee shop dropped something and made a noise.

Reality made a strong comeback.

The happiness that had twinkled in our eyes seconds ago began to settle down as we became aware of our surroundings.

'You know what else I had imagined?' he asked me. There was something magical in the atmosphere, in the air between us. I welcomed the pain. I found happiness in it for it was going to be about us. It was going to be about how he felt for me.

'Tell me . . .' I said softly. And just then tears rolled down my cheeks.

He looked at me, unmoved. He knew the difficult phase we were in. So he let me sob.

He chose to keep talking, 'I'd imagined going on vacations with you . . . Holding your hand and walking on the seashore as the sun went down, with the waves kissing our feet. The two of us watching the sun dipping into the sea and disappearing into the horizon, as the thin line of golden light that separates the sea from the sky appeared. And when darkness would take over, I would hold you tightly in my arms. And now that I have seen you in that red dress, in my updated imagination I see you wearing it. I'd bury my face in your neck, inhaling your scent. I would imagine that you are mine. I so wanted to believe . . .'

He could not finish. His eyes told the rest of the story. Aarav didn't even bother to wipe off his tears. I shared his imagination by imagining him wearing the same suit that he wore when I saw him in the salon a few months back.

We were hopelessly in love. We could not help ourselves, or each other.

Aarav's love for me wasn't physical. I could see that. And that made him even more desirable.

The next moment, I saw him smiling. He was thinking about something. He recalled a few things from the past. He told me how awestruck he was to see me by chance in the sports bra that day in the store. I laughed at that. I was laughing and crying at the same time.

'I secretly desired to see you again like that.' I too shared with him how though it had happened by accident that I too didn't mind him seeing me like that. We recalled many such moments and eventually rolled back in time to my first mistake—when I rammed my car into his.

There came a moment when Aarav could not resist saying, 'Why can't I have you in my life, Naina?' He hit the table with his knuckles and hurt himself. I immediately held his hand and rubbed it in between my palms.

We were caught in a chaos of emotions with pain dominating every feeling.

How had we landed here?

It all flashed in my mind. All that he had told me, as we stood in that parking lot. So much had happened between us and we were letting go of so much. Aarav stepped closer and hugged me. It felt good to be in his arms. I held him tight. 'Naina!' he said. I looked up into his eyes. Then I couldn't help myself and reached out to kiss him. It was as if he had been waiting for a sign from me. He pulled me in and kissed me energetically. Aarav crossed the line that he had marked for himself. And yet it appeared just the right thing to do. Perhaps it had to do with our final goodbye that was due in a couple of seconds. I ran my fingers through his hair and caressed his neck and back; I wanted to get lost in his arms or take him in mine. When slowly we separated, we were full of the realization that it was our last kiss. A love story that witnesses its first and last kiss in the same week is often forgettable. But ours was special. We were going to remember it forever.

Again, we stood apart. Nothing to say, but so much between us! Words fell short to express what we were going through. And therefore, for a while, there was only silence. A silence that kept reminding us that it would all be over very soon.

'I . . . I will leave now . . .'

I knew that was coming. I was there to hear those words. I was prepared. And yet, when I heard them, I felt they stabbed my chest. I felt this sudden heaviness in my heart. I felt weak and helpless. At times the short space between understanding reality and accepting it turns out to be the most difficult to walk.

I opened my mouth to say something. But not a word came out of it.

'Goodbye,' he said.

I could barely nod my head. 'Good . . . goodbye,' I said.

He smiled a lost smile and turned to leave. And as he walked in the direction of his car, away from me, I wished I could freeze time. I wished I could run and hold him. I couldn't do either. I just stood there and watched him go away from me.

How could I imagine living without him now? How could I go back to being the same Naina when he'd touched me the way no one had? It didn't feel wrong to be in his arms, to kiss him—it felt just right. The way I felt for Aarav, I'd never felt for anyone. I was married to Siddharth but I loved Aarav. That was the first time I understood how if it is love, it always feels right.

As he walked away from me I felt he was taking away a part of me, something that belonged to me, forever. And I could do nothing about it. And then it all became blurry. Sometimes I feel tears have a mind of their own. They intervene and try to disconnect your vision from the element of pain.

Twenty-four

'But what about the infidelity aspect of an extramarital affair? Doesn't that make you feel guilty?'

After a long time, Manvika and I were together again in the steam room. For days, I didn't come to the gym after Aarav had left. But Manvika insisted that I must visit. She understood my emotional condition and feared that I was suffering from depression. Sid had extended his trip. Confined in my bedroom, I had been crying all this while.

Manvika wanted me to change course. She kept checking on me regularly. I too desired her company and more so because Aarav was a common link between us.

'I am not going to get a new personal trainer. How about the two of us work out together from now onwards,' she had suggested the evening before.

I had agreed and hence I was with her.

We end up continuing with the very discussion which I had left in the middle of one evening at Manvika's house. With nobody around us, we were again in the privacy of each other's company.

'Infidelity is when you hide your other relationship from your spouse,' Manvika calmly said stretching her legs on the wet slab.

'What? You mean . . .' I stammered.

Manvika didn't need me to complete the question either. 'Yes,' she said.

I was shocked to realize that all this while I believed that she was cheating on her husband.

But now, I was more bothered by the ease with which she had admitted than what she had admitted. In the time that had passed since our last discussion, I had retracted a bit on my newly found position. Away from Manvika's proximity and back in my typical world, the influence of Manvika's words over me had worn off a bit. Acknowledging a change is one thing, accepting it is another.

Changing one's mindset requires time.

What kind of marriage is this then? I wondered.

Manvika's revelation left me disturbed. I couldn't fathom what was more disturbing. That she was in an extramarital relationship? Or, that her husband knew about the fact that she was in an extramarital relationship?

Or was I overreacting? Given that my own extramarital relationship had come to an end.

But when there is nothing to hide from your spouse, there is no question of infidelity. The point of adultery was bothering me the most ever since the two of us had first discussed this subject. Now that this whole plot of cheating had vanished, I had lost my reference point. I needed some time to think through and reflect. Besides, for a moment I realized I was more wrong than Manvika; Manvika was not practising adultery; I was. In my mind, the truth was turned on its head.

'What happened?' Manvika asked when she didn't hear anything from me. Thick steam had engulfed both of us. I didn't know why, but I felt it helped my situation a bit.

Then it struck me and I asked, 'So you don't love your husband?'

Through the white vapours hanging in the air between us, I heard Manvika giggle at my statement. 'I do,' she finally said.

Her laugh helped me calm down a bit, but her answer didn't connect the dots for me. It gave birth to more questions. Manvika had become a fascinating mystery that I found myself involved in solving. The more I flipped the pages of her mind, the more complex she became. And the best part was— she welcomed me at every page and never once asked me to back off.

When she didn't hear a response from me, she spoke, 'When you are in an extramarital relationship people either think there is something wrong in your relationship or with you. This may not always be right. It's not, in my case.'

'And you are perfectly fine if your husband seeks a similar relationship outside marriage?' I asked back.

'I will be a hypocrite to deny him the same freedom.'

So, I followed up with my question, 'Then what kind of marriage is this?'

Even though my question was an open-ended one, Manvika understood what I meant. She said she could understand all that was going on in my mind and offered me an explanation. 'My husband and I are social beings who live together, under one roof, because we want to live together. Neither of us binds the other and makes him or her live by a certain set of rules. If anything, the rule is of freedom; respecting that even though we stay together, we may have different tastes and different expectations from life. Marriage, to us, is a commitment of sharing lives. Not being caged or controlling each other . . .'

And in that low-visibility steam-laden room, as if with her words, Manvika held my hand and yet again walked me into a different world of marriage that I was unacquainted with. I realized how beautifully she described marriage in her words . . . *that a husband and wife are two social beings who have come to live together . . . that marriage is a commitment to share each other's lives, not to control each other.* I wondered why I never looked at marriage in this manner. It was such a refreshing viewpoint.

'. . . We weren't like this when we got married to each other. It all happened by and by. And I am glad that we frankly spoke about it to each other, instead of hiding it. One night, we were out for dinner and he was the first one to bring up this matter over drinks. He spoke his mind. He said he was getting attracted to a colleague. Initially, I did feel vulnerable and insecure. It took me some time to settle down. I recalled how at times, I too underwent similar moments at my work place. I was glad he was man enough to say it to me. As a woman, I could not honestly voice my feeling. Yet, he was sure he still loved me. I was sure he did; I could see that in his eyes. Else, he would not have shared this with me.

'That evening, time and again I thought about my husband's confession, I gave more importance to the fact that he hadn't cheated on me. He could have easily done that. There was no need for him to let me know. At the same time, I also wondered about what if he had not told me about this?

'What all amounts to adultery? Is it just the physical acts? Or, even imagining Tom Cruise when your husband is making love to you reeks of adultery? And if that's the case, then how do I curb his thoughts? Can I curb my own thoughts? Is it possible? Do we even need to do so? The more I thought over, the more I realized that I couldn't. I learned to let go.

'And guess what? When I set him free, his love for me grew like never before. I not only saw it, I felt it, every day. That night as we drove back home, I asked him why he chose to speak to me, when he could have hidden it and cheated on me. He told me something unbelievably beautiful. He said, *I would have failed our marriage, if I had not opened up to the very person with whom I share my life. I want my wife to be my best friend, with whom I can share anything and everything.* I think there is no better way to put what he said then. That's his primary expectation from me—to be his best friend. Today, we reciprocate the same freedom and same love for each other. It has strengthened our relationship. And therefore, my biggest learning from my marriage has been—love does not bind you. Love sets you free. Love flourishes in freedom. If you see marriage as the end of freedom, you are doing it wrong,' she said.

It all sounded sensible, and magical!

Manvika paused and then continued, '. . . look around us to see how we perceive marriage. This *ab-to-shaadi-ho-chuki-hai* approach. The whole THIS-IS-IT!-now-live-with-it attitude curtails the openness. This idea of finality, which is intrinsic to marriage is enough to throw me off. Why do you think the new generation is hesitant to get married and they keep delaying it as far as possible? Why do you think divorces are rampant? Unlike earlier, when divorces brought along a sense of shame, now they bring in a sense of freedom. How's it wrong if a couple agrees to bring this very freedom into their marriage and save themselves the trouble of splitting up? I refuse to see marriage as a restrained institution.'

Manvika's words were revolutionary. They offered me an unfamiliar perspective into marriage, one that has been seldom highlighted. At least, not this brazenly!

'But then why does this freedom sound so immoral? So unethical?' I asked.

'Because we have been conditioned to believe this way. We have been brought up in society this way. This thought of not being right is the social conditioning one needs to get over. I want a logical sense to it. I want something that fits scientifically and systematically. I don't want to follow what society says, just because I grew up learning that.'

She wasn't done yet.

'Unfortunately, our society has romanticized the idea of living in denial rather than acknowledging complexities. We avoid confrontations, so we go the easy way—Condemn it! Deny it! We are scared to introspect and find answers to the logical questions. We hide our feelings but, for not for once, we ask the legitimate question—why do we feel this way in the first place? This attraction beyond the so-called forbidden lines? Why is it everywhere today?'

I thought of Aarav in that moment. Manvika could not notice my facial expressions. She went on.

'Why do we deny this feeling? Why are we ashamed of accepting something that happens naturally to us? Why do we attach a stigma to it and therefore keep it under a veil, hide it from the world and curse ourselves? Why do we have to cheat on our partners? And if not that, then why do we have to suppress our real feelings? Instead, why can't we be open about them? Express them and see if we can cherish them without guilt?'

In the light of her jaw-dropping statements, Manvika's elaborate reasoning again influenced my views. I was amused how every time, she would initially appear so wrong to me. But by the end of her explanation I would get around to see her point of view.

Manvika's assessment of marriage had the vital element of absolute freedom in it, which is missing in the society we live in. From where I could see now, Manvika was quite right for she breathed in freedom, in the air of happiness. Besides, she too was not in favour of adultery, something I believed she was till then. In that aspect, Manvika was much like Aarav. Irrespective of the fact that these two people were so diverse in their thoughts on relationships, their idea of not wanting a relationship that appeared like a sin and brought guilt to their conscience positioned them at the same level in my mind. *Yet how different they were from each other!* On one hand, was Aarav, a man who seldom crossed the line to even touch me inappropriately, though he had every opportunity to do so. And on the other was Manvika, a woman, who justified the fulfilment of all her desires. In their hearts they were both right.

I realized I wasn't done with my questions yet. It was a brand new Manvika I was in conversation with. And listening to her thoughts with an open mind, I was discovering a brand new me.

'I had never thought the way you think, Manvika. The way you look at a marriage. And I would have to say that on logical grounds, I agree with you. However, there is this one thing. And I wonder, in spite of all your reasoning, why the idea of having sex outside marriage appears disturbingly difficult to me. How are you so comfortable with it, even if your husband reciprocates by awarding you equal freedom?'

'Because in my mind I don't treat sex as oh-my-God-SEX! I don't consider sex to be outside my idea of freedom!

Having said that, my definition of freedom in marriage is not limited to the freedom of having sex outside marriage, but a lot of things beyond it. It could be partying out till late in the night with colleagues who are men and not being judged. It could be living alone in a different country for a while. The freedom to decide whether or not we both want kids and not just produce them because only he wants or because that's what others expect out of us. There are many such issues. But now that you have mentioned only this three-letter word, let me tell you that I consider sex as an extremely important aspect of life. It's a powerful energy and a driving force. I crave for it. I enjoy it. Consensual sex is a simple act driven by nature. We humans have made it an ethical and a moral issue, attached shame and disgrace to it. We have complicated it.'

Even though Manvika's words were reasonable, strangely, at times, I found them difficult to digest. Somewhere at the back of my mind, I still looked for reasons to counter them. That's the thing with social conditioning. When you are brought up in a certain way, to believe certain things, to practise certain things, you find it really hard to believe otherwise—even if the opposite is rational and your belief is superficial. You wonder why then you have believed something all this while. You introspect. And that's when the real change within you kicks in.

As I continued to debate aloud what was now in my conscience, something struck Manvika and she chuckled. 'You know, last night I was watching this movie, *The Holiday*. And in one passionate scene Cameron Diaz says to Jude Law, "Sex complicates things."'

'Okay?'

'And Jude tells her, "But we didn't have it." To which Cameron says, "It complicates in any form. Not having it also complicates things."'

I laughed appreciating the beauty with which the dialogue writer had put forth the argument. It made so much sense.

'I guess you are right. We humans have really distorted something simple into something complicated,' I conceded.

'The truth, Naina, is simple—humans are polygamous. But the fact that we tend to confine humans into one relationship and mark his or her territory—it complicates things.'

'Let me ask you this then. So when you are in love with more than one man at the same time . . .'

I wasn't even finished when Manvika interrupted.

'Correction!' she said and added, 'I am in love with only one man and that's my husband. The rest is attraction.'

I was taken aback and so I asked, 'And how do you differentiate between the two?'

Interestingly, Manvika had a simple answer to this. 'I won't make similar sacrifices for someone who I am attracted to, as I would for somebody who I am in love with.'

'Sacrifices like?'

'Mmm . . . like leaving my parents to come to live with him. My husband changed his geographical location and moved here because my work demands it and he didn't mind taking a transfer in his company to their office in Gurgaon. Sacrifices are mutual here . . . you see! And we did so because we love each other and we wanted to live with each other.'

'Fair point!' For once, someone offered me a litmus test to find out whether you are in love or if it is just an attraction. The test of sacrifices!

'But is it possible for one person to be in love with two different people, at the same time?'

'It is.'

But I wasn't satisfied with it. So I asked, 'Is it not strange?'

'That we find it strange—is strange to me,' Manvika chuckled and said. 'Have you ever realized we don't find it strange how a mother is equally in love with all her children? We never find it strange when a person shares love with more than one person in any other relationship, as long as it is not a romantic one. Only in the latter case we find it strange. Isn't *that* strange?'

'True! But . . . given . . . aaa . . . that you know . . . that attraction isn't love . . . would you . . . still allow it?'

'It's not in my hands to control attraction, Naina. Attraction does not take my permission.'

The two of us burst out laughing.

'Attraction is just natural. Just like love. Even the gods and the king of gods, Indra, haven't been spared of its effect. He disguised as sage Gautama and had sex with the latter's wife, Ahalya. He even sent Menaka to earth to seduce sage Vishwamitra and succeeded in breaking his meditation because the ascetic got attracted to Menaka. This world of Ahalya and Menaka, this world of *deva*s like Indra and *rishi*s like Vishwamitra, this world of attraction, this so-called world of adultery has been in existence since that age. You see! It's that powerful. And look at us! Mere mortals! The school of infidelity came into existence the day the institution of marriage was invented. Extramarital affairs in the human civilization are going to continue till the concept of marriage survives. That you desire to be with someone but can't have him or her in fullness keeps the flame of desire burning. This desire is its own fuel, you see! How do you douse it? Perhaps it's this journey of continuously desiring that's far more thrilling than the final destination of being with someone forever. Attraction doesn't recognize boundaries. All I want is a world where an Indra doesn't have to disguise as Gautama any more. All I want is a world where an Ahalya isn't cursed to become a stone any more. I want a world where we acknowledge that attractions are just normal and we accept them.'

'Do you think society will ever approve of it?'

'Society!' Manvika mocked and paused.

She resumed, 'Well, society didn't approve of the first person who claimed the world is round and not flat. Society laughed at that person. It took its sweet time. That's the thing with society. It shows resistance. It doesn't like change. But the truth is that over a period of time, it has to change. And till then, it gives immense credibility to what it had continued to believe; even if it may not have done anything to scientifically verify its own stand. It hurts our society real bad, when you question its belief system. Besides, who exactly do we call society—the majority of mankind, living in a certain arrangement and adhering to certain common viewpoints? So no, society won't approve of it in the initial phase. But some individuals will! The logical ones will. And the day these individuals are in the majority, they will form a new society.'

'You think so?' I wondered if we could ever become that liberal.

'What do you mean I think so? Dumbo! It's happening. It's a work in progress. Lot of things have happened. A lot are yet to happen.'

'What has changed?'

'Today society agrees that the world is round,' Manvika promptly answered.

The two of us again broke into a big laugh. It was a much-needed one given the intensity with which we held that discussion. It felt good to laugh after what felt like a long while, ever since Aarav had left. How Manvika's company made me feel comfortable and not miss Aarav as badly as I did back at my home.

Manvika spoke again, 'No, but seriously, a lot has happened and a lot is happening. We are in a social transition. More than half a century ago, sati was practiced in this country. Widows were burnt alive. That's what the then society believed in. Today there are widow remarriages happening in our society. Just imagine the transition—from those so-called ethical murders of widows to re-establishing happiness in their lives. See, how this very society has come a long way. Today we are fighting to establish social acceptance of homosexuality. Yesterday there were fewer voices. Today there are many. If so many can now accept, that what once they believed was unnatural, one day society will accept what we are talking about today. After all, a relationship outside a relationship may be seen as forbidden, but it is still not seen as unnatural.' Manvika ended with a laugh.

I had always known about sati. But it had remained in my subconscious mind. Who would have believed that one day we would be fighting for the right of a man to legally marry another man? I never looked at it the way Manvika used it to point out the drastic change in the mindset of our society. Indeed, in the light of this evolution of our culture, Manvika's views on the institution of marriage didn't appear that alien any more. After all, she was not endorsing adultery, but open marriages.

Manvika got up and redraped her towel. I realized that I had lost track of time. It had been a long, deep conversation. I didn't know how much time had passed.

'Shall we?' Manvika asked as she faced the glass door.

I nodded. I didn't have any more questions left. By then she had answered them all.

That afternoon, in the steam room, Manvika had certainly changed my perspective of looking at married life. And I knew that it was a definite change—one that needed no more verifications or validation. I knew that her definition of marriage was going to stay for an eternity in my mind—it is a commitment to share your lives, not to control each other.

Epilogue

It's been eight months now since Aarav left for Canada. His going away was not the end of our relationship. We continue to be in touch. We were and are in love! There is no denying that.

He went away from me to restrict chances of moving further into the dangerous waters of love. We were both aware that it would bring its fair share of regret.

I had hated Aarav when he had left me. It had depressed me beyond my tolerance. I cried quietly for a long time. But at the back of my mind, even then, and more so now, I had immense respect for him for being somebody who valued his conscience, when I had gone against my own. That only proved that I had fallen in love with the right guy.

It amuses me to recall how almost a year and a half back I had bumped into two individuals, who ended up changing my life, completely. Who, back then, would have thought that Aarav and Manvika would have served such a huge purpose in my life? How the dots connected! One brought in the much-needed love I had longed for in my life. The other propelled me to come out of the limbo of an unwanted life. I was stuck in. Manvika showed me that I deserved better and that changed everything for me.

While one gave me a reason to move on, the other showed me how to move on.

Aarav had left because he also felt that his proximity to me would never allow me to think straight and take a call on my life. This is where Manvika filled in the gap. The two of us have had numerous discussions on the subject of relationships. We touched upon and discussed every aspect of it—love, sex, relationship, marriage and a lot beyond that as well.

In the end it all boiled down to one thing—happiness; my happiness!

Aarav's absence and Manvika's presence helped me decide things for myself in an unbiased manner. In the days that followed Aarav's departure, I pulled up myself to stand for what was right for me, for the kind of relationship I wanted to be in and the life I wanted to live.

I had a few heart-to-heart conversations with Sid in which I expressed how I felt suffocated in our relationship. The purpose was not to begin a blame game but to see if we could change things; to see if my marriage could become a fulfilling experience for me as well. But my confession to Siddharth that in the years we had spent together, I'd never felt complete, did more harm than good. It hurt his male ego.

During this time, I also introspected if I loved Sid enough. And I found an honest answer in my heart. Not that I didn't make an effort to love Sid, but when I didn't see him reciprocating, I gradually slipped in my efforts too. That's one big difference between trying to love and falling in love, I guess.

My talks with my husband didn't give the results I was looking for. My aim to set new expectations for us, as a couple, only further irritated Siddharth. At times he even became aggressive, a reaction I had never seen before. The basic expectations appeared *new* to him because by then he was happily settled with the status quo. He didn't want to change the equation, bring a learning curve and do something that didn't come naturally to him. He derived love from his business. It fulfilled him.

My first big stand came when one night I rejected the idea of having our baby. Not that I didn't want a child, but not at that time; not when I was contemplating the course of my life. And from there on began my fight to build my happy life.

I wasn't demanding the moon. I was asking for very fundamental, very basic things. Having known Manvika so closely, I began drawing parallels between our respective lives. While she was fulfilling her wants, my point of debate with Sid was that he had left my needs unfulfilled. But then you can't push someone to love you. Love is not a formality. It has to come from inside. It did not come to Siddharth and he saw no reason to try.

Things didn't work out between Sid and me. As a result of which the subsequent discussions we had were not just between the two of us. First it was Manvika who joined us for a talk. By then Sid had got to know about my equation with Aarav. Manvika helped me share this with him. It was difficult. But Manvika had taught me to be honest and transparent. Then there were my parents with whom I had shared my thoughts. From denying the existence of a problem in the first place to acknowledging that there's one, they had come a long way. It was quite difficult for them to even understand what I was saying. *What was wrong in my marriage?* Here, as well, Manvika helped me in making them understand what I was going through. And then came the phase when they prepared themselves to sit and talk over this with everyone. Eventually, they did come to my side. The last conversation we had involved both our families. Manvika wasn't a part of this.

'From here on you will have to fight your own battle,' she had told me.

I will never be able to thank Manvika enough for coming into my life, showing me the way and bolstering me to stand for myself.

In the all-family meet, my final words were shockingly deafening to everyone, and more so, to Sid. I felt week before I spoke them. A number of times I even contemplated if I should not make myself go through all that I had to say. I felt scared. I felt I wouldn't be able to do it. I wanted to give up. But right at that moment, I recalled Aarav's words: *If you give up before reaching the finishing line, how will you get to know if there was a miracle awaiting you right there? So keep moving even if you are tired, even if you are far behind. Beyond this, glory is awaiting you. Don't give up. It's going to hurt, but if you give up now, it's going to hurt forever!*

'I want to move out of this marriage,' I had said.

What followed was a depressing silence. But I knew beyond this horrible silence stood my happiness.

When relationships break they cause pain. But then a short-term pain is better for a long-term and larger good. Besides, this pain for the two families had more to do with societal pressure—of what people will say when they get to know this. I was long done with caring for society.

In my mind, I was clear on one thing—just like everybody lived the life they wanted to live, I too deserved the right to live the life I wanted to live. It was only fair.

As I finish writing this story, Siddharth and my separation is on its way. I still believe he is a gentleman and a good human being. He just couldn't become a good husband; or logically speaking, and as Manvika would have said, he couldn't become the kind of husband I needed.

I wanted to be with Aarav. But the twist in my story is that I didn't quit my marriage to be with Aarav. I quit because I realized it wasn't right for me to be in a wrong relationship. As time passed by, I also became aware of the mistakes I had made in the past to land up in the marriage I was now leaving. To be mature is to be cautious, not to make a similar mistake in a new way. As of now, even though I still want to be with Aarav, I am thinking over it. For, years later, I don't want to break any more hearts or get a broken heart myself. And as I think over this, I again go back to the long conversations between Manvika and me.

We each had our perspectives to look at love and relationships. Even though there were a good number of overlaps, there were certain differences as well.

I respected Manvika's opinion. I derived a lot of strength from her. Yet, I built my own opinions. After all, we are two different individuals. Manvika is a logical person. Logic comes naturally to her. I am more of an emotional person.

In my case, emotions are the first priority. Therefore, while I agreed with her argument to do away with societal conditioning, I also realized I won't be able to escape my basic nature at an individual level. On that ground, I found it difficult to imagine that I could share the person I loved with somebody else. It felt like splitting a part of me and giving it away. My heart wanted to follow my love. It was never looking for logic. That's where my happiness lay.

We both agreed on the concept of individual freedom in a relationship. The only differences in our mind were related to its degree. And the more we talked about it the more we stood our grounds—not to convince the other person, but to convince ourselves. While, honestly speaking, there was no need for Manvika to convince herself, our conversations were more of introspections for me to find out the right grounds for my happiness.

In my view, there should be a degree to the freedom that couples agree upon.

'Freedom that is not absolute, is not freedom in the true sense,' Manvika would say.

Technically she was right. The moment we attach a degree to freedom, we compromise the true meaning of freedom.

In the end, both of us agreed that there was no right or wrong position in this. That's the reason we were not able to end our discussions. Ultimately, it depends on the two individuals who are going to live together. If they are both very possessive of each other and don't want to share each other with anyone, then that's good for them. If the two want to be in an open relationship and it suites them, then it's good for them.

But I still don't know what happens if one person expects more freedom and the other is not willing to give that. Problems would creep in for sure. I shudder to think that if some day I am with Aarav and I have to share him with somebody else. *What will I do then?*

I am not very sure. *Will I stop him?* I would not have wanted Siddharth to stop me from seeing Aarav. Manvika didn't stop her husband. Her point was that you can only stop a person physically, you can't dictate his mind. *Will I be able to control Aarav's mind?* I don't know.

Knowing Aarav's principles on the subject of adultery, there are higher chances he won't hide it. But then life has taught me that anything can happen. What if he doesn't even hide but honestly tells me that he is attracted to somebody else, just like Manvika and her husband had shared everything. What will I do then?

I don't know yet. Perhaps, if that day comes, I will go back to Manvika's words—love means to let go! Even if I may not want to, I might have to. Yet I need more time to get a clear understanding of this. I don't want to rush into a new beginning with Aarav till I find my own answers.

But this doesn't take away from the fact that I am in love with Aarav. And that this is the first time I have truly fallen in love.

Author's Question

Hello reader,

Now that you have read this story, I have a question for you. Not that you are obliged to answer me. But I will be grateful to you, if you do so. I will keep my question brief.

Both Naina and Manvika were in extramarital relationships.

My question to you is: Who do you agree with more? Naina, who thinks the idea of love outside a relationship is not right and yet lands up in that very situation? Or Manvika, who has an extramarital affair but does not hide it from her spouse?

You can write to me (preferably) on my Twitter handle or on my Facebook page. You will find these contact details in my bio-note in beginning of this book.

Acknowledgements

My sincere thanks to the following people who helped me finish writing this book and/or assisted me with their views and feedback on the subject.

Vaishali Mathur, my commissioning editor at Penguin Random House, for being with me throughout my journey of writing this story. The lengthy discussions we held on our really long drive from Delhi to Dehradun helped this book. For going through the entire story multiple number of times to improve the quality of the manuscript. More importantly, just like for some of my other books, for helping me conceive the title. How we end up spending days to finalize these 4–5 words, always!

Paloma Dutta, my copy editor at Penguin Random House, for editing and making the entire manuscript presentable. For being patient with me while I kept shuffling the sequence of chapters.

Debashreeta Mishra, my friend, for sharing her perspective with me. Naina and Manvika's discussions over the subject of love, sex and the school of marriage, which I believe are key chapters in this book, are an outcome of our continuous conversations on this subject.

Ananth Padmanabhan and Nikita Singh, my friends from the world of books, for going through the key chapters in this book at my request, and getting back to me with their views on them. Glad I reached out to you folks.

The numerous anonymous readers of my books, who wrote to me with confessions of being in multiple relationships at the same time. They wrote that they wanted to share the secret of their affairs with me for, in some way, it reduced their guilt. Thank you for trusting me, even though I couldn't be of any help to you.

Last, but not the least, my wife Khushboo Chauhan, with whom I first talked about the subject of this story. For sharing with me real-life stories of people who landed up in extramarital relationships and how that broke their marriages. For not once judging them, but apprising me of their behavioural changes, their emotional states and their states of mind. For showing confidence in me about writing on this topic.